I Once Stood

Franklin Jon Zuch

an imprint of Sunbury Press, Inc.
Mechanicsburg, PA USA

MILFORD HOUSE

an imprint of Sunbury Press, Inc.
Mechanicsburg, PA USA

NOTE: This is a work of fiction. Names, characters, places, and incidents either are the product of the author's imagination or are used fictitiously. While, as in all fiction, the literary perceptions and insights are shaped by experiences, any resemblance to actual persons, living or dead, events, or locales is entirely coincidental.

Copyright © 2025 by Franklin Jon Zuch.
Cover Copyright © 2025 by Sunbury Press, Inc.

Sunbury Press supports copyright. Copyright fuels creativity, encourages diverse voices, promotes free speech, and creates a vibrant culture. Thank you for buying an authorized edition of this book and for complying with copyright laws. Except for the quotation of short passages for the purpose of criticism and review, no part of this publication may be reproduced, scanned, or distributed in any form without permission. You are supporting writers and allowing Sunbury Press to continue to publish books for every reader. For information contact Sunbury Press, Inc., Subsidiary Rights Dept., PO Box 548, Boiling Springs, PA 17007 USA or legal@sunburypress.com.

For information about special discounts for bulk purchases, please contact Sunbury Press Orders Dept. at (855) 338-8359 or orders@sunburypress.com.

To request one of our authors for speaking engagements or book signings, please contact Sunbury Press Publicity Dept. at publicity@sunburypress.com.

FIRST MILFORD HOUSE PRESS EDITION: January 2025

Set in Adobe Garamond Pro | Interior design by Crystal Devine | Cover by Lawrence Knorr | Edited by Anaya Montgomery.

Publisher's Cataloging-in-Publication Data
Names: Zuch, Franklin Jon, author.
Title: I once stood / Franklin Jon Zuch.
Description: First trade paperback edition. | Mechanicsburg, PA : Milford House Press, 2025.
Summary: The story of a man in the eighteenth century colonial American as relayed through a journal that was given to him on his eighteenth birthday by his father. Further information would ruin the surprise ending.
Identifiers: ISBN : 979-8-88819-279-5 (paperback).
Subjects: FICTION / Historical / Colonial America & Revolution | FICTION / Historical / General | FICTION / General.

Designed in the USA
0 1 1 2 3 5 8 13 21 34 55

For the Love of Books!

Dedicated to the unsung heroes of the American Revolution, whose stories will never be told. Many of these patriots are anonymously buried in Philadelphia's Washington Square, which features a statue of General George Washington, an eternal flame, and the Tomb of the Unknown Soldier. The soldier was designated American due to the plain metal jacket buttons versus the larger, more ornate British red coat uniform buttons. The inscription on the monument reads: "FREEDOM IS A LIGHT FOR WHICH MANY MEN HAVE DIED IN DARKNESS"

Prologue

In all its distant explosive fury, the sun rose slowly and silently above the spring green canopy of the Virginia woodlands. After an initial bright green flash, it took a full three minutes for the flaming, orange sphere, shimmering in the atmosphere, to snap free from the horizon below. The first penetrating rays glistened in the dew-covered ferns thriving in the ancient humus. The night had yielded to the astronomical, nautical, and civil twilights and the first two golden hours of the day had begun. The forest was ablaze with exquisite color and filled with the vibrant sounds of nature. The white and pink dogwood trees were a perfect backdrop for the yellow daffodils and the forsythia bushes, which were attracting the chirping goldfinches flittering about. The male goldfinch's plumage is a drab olive gray in the winter and molts bright yellow in the spring and summer to attract a mate. As the first sign of spring, the small blooming crocus plants add bright accents to the sprouting green ferns and the glowing purple wisteria vines naturally know which lackluster trees to adorn. A robin was singing a beautiful song to claim his nesting territory, while acknowledging and respecting the songs of other robins staking their own claims nearby. A small herd of deer was calmly enjoying their morning feast of berries and bark, after an unusually long, cold, and wet winter. Suddenly, the tranquility of this peaceful setting was interrupted by a piercing scream from an unknown source. The deer instantly raised their heads and set their ears in the direction of the intrusion. At the second cry, they bounded over the underbrush into the forest, with their white undertails flashing the alert.

The disturbance was coming from a log cabin situated in a glen featuring a swift-moving creek and a good-sized tobacco field that would go unattended on this particular day in May 1738. Inside, William Ambruster, a short, stocky, but powerfully built farmer comforted his wife Mary, who had just given birth to a protesting boy. He was now crying out and eagerly trying to focus on his new surroundings. He had been pulled from a safe and warm existence into a world that would provide the inevitable experiences, good and bad, that all living beings endure. Their firstborn, Sarah, two years old, the only other child of Mary and William, watched as her parents held the newborn and exulted in the success of the birth. Having already miscarried two babies, they had agreed on one last attempt for a son, to carry on the Ambruster name that would otherwise die with William. They named him Philip, with the middle name Winemore, after Mary's maiden name.

Philip's early childhood was spent exploring the woods, with its wildlife of birds, frogs, lizards, squirrels, and other wonders of nature that held no particular significance to his family. They couldn't understand why he would spend so much time traipsing through the woods eating Jack-in-the-Pulpit root bulbs and whacking skunk cabbage with a stick. Philip was particularly fascinated by the annual migration of the monarch butterflies every September. He would be astounded if he knew that it takes five generations to fly north from Mexico to as far away as Canada before returning south to the forested central highlands for the winter.

Every evening featured nightly lessons and Philip always sat next to Sarah, a surrogate mother of sorts, since their mother was always inundated with the chores of a frontier woman. Although William worked the earth, he put much of his energy into the education of his children. When he summoned them shortly after dinner, they both came willingly and enthusiastically. These nights were comfortable, with the crackling, blazing fire on the hearth casting flickering shadows throughout the room. As she completed her daily routine, Mary listened to her devoted husband as he lectured their children on reading, writing, arithmetic, and history, including family history. William did have some Shakspearian books and other published resources passed down through the generations from his English ancestors. Still, for the most part, the makeshift school's lessons came from handwritten notebooks he had prepared. He also used the Ambruster family Bible, journals, and assorted diaries that thoughtful relatives had loyally updated over the years. Philip was most interested in his family history and he purposely committed as much as he could to memory.

***

The first American Ambrusters were charter members of the Virginia Company of London simply referred to as the London Company. This was a group of explorers, with a common goal of finding gold and silver in the New World. Most of the initial expeditions venturing out from England to lands far away did not attract much attention from investors, until incredible stories of American wealth started circulating. The joint stock companies finally began to lure support of the merchants, whose money funded these overseas enterprises. One such investor, Daniel Ambruster, who not only contributed his life savings, but also boarded the ship AMPHORA, with his wife Emma, and all the belongings they could carry. After a harrowing four-month journey, Daniel and his wife, along with 102 other brave and ambitious souls, on three tiny ships, sailed up the James River in Virginia. It was late in 1607 when they began to build a small town, naming it Jamestown in honor of their king. With the leadership of John Smith and adventurous farmers like John Rolfe and Daniel Ambruster, this first permanent English settlement in America was established, thirteen years before the Pilgrims were to land at Plymouth. These original Jamestown residents failed in their quest for gold and silver but succeeded in cultivating cash crops. One species of tobacco named Imperial Weed, grown from seeds from the West Indies, became their main source of income.

Life at Jamestown was brutal, and more than four hundred people died the first winter. The survivors persisted until 1609, when attacks by the Algonquian tribe, rampant disease, and famine brought the settlement to the brink of total failure, They were saved by the arrival of two ships with a cache of supplies and a new governor, Lord De La Warr. A small group of the surviving settlers, including Daniel Ambruster, together with recent arrivals, decided to abandon Jamestown and forged west to establish a new settlement named Middle Plantation. It would flourish and eventually be renamed Williamsburg, which would replace Jamestown as the colonial capital in 1699. Generations of Ambrusters would go on to grow the broadleaved species of tobacco, as their major export to the English market. The latest adult Ambruster generation, William and his older brother Thomas, continued the family tradition of farming on their forefathers' farm until August 1735, when William married Mary Winemore. It soon became obvious that the farmhouse was too small for the newlyweds, Thomas, Elizabeth, and their three children. After much consternation, they sold the farm and split the proceeds. Thomas used his share to book one-way passage to Boston as his wife wanted to reunite with her family, and hopefully, he would secure a position in the Geddy family business. William, with farming in his blood, chose to homestead one of the available claims in the western frontier of Virginia. After digging up hundreds of seedlings, he loaded them into his wagon, with a plow and other tools, and set out with Mary for the sparsely inhabited, and largely uncharted, Virginia wilderness. Fortunately, three of William's single friends accompanied the Ambrusters to the site of their new beginning and spent a month constructing a cabin, with building materials brought in from Williamsburg. It was a solid home, with shuttered windows, wooden shingles, a strong door, and a plank floor, above a sizable cellar for storage. They also built a primitive barn, more like a shed, for the horses and to dry the harvested tobacco. At the end of that first year, December 1736, they were blessed with the birth of their first child Sarah and their first crop of tobacco.

***

Now, with the birth of Philip, the Ambrusters enlarged their living space with a new addition in the New England saltbox style. It would contain two bedrooms, one for Sarah and one for the parents, with Philip remaining in the loft of the original cabin. A second fireplace dominated the center of the addition's common room floor, with a brick chimney extending through the roof. With the help of fellow homesteaders, they also built a larger barn with rows of drying racks to accommodate the increased yield from the extended tobacco fields.

As Philip grew, his chores increased. When he reached the age of twelve, his responsibilities were expanded to include working the plow, chopping firewood, and helping with the tobacco harvest. He was not on his father's sunup to sundown schedule, but it was back-breaking work, nonetheless. His father always stressed that a strong mind, with a strong back, makes the man. William also stressed the importance to listen to your heart, follow your gut, and be true to yourself. He impressed upon Philip that, although he was being raised on a farm, he didn't have to stick to the land. He regularly enticed Philip with lively stories, such as the goings on in Williamsburg. Some lessons included maps that his father would prepare to distant places, such as Uncle Thomas' city of Boston. Philip would climb the ladder mounted to the wall and retreat to his loft in the peak of the cabin's roof to study these maps and dream of the future. As his parents and sister slept on the ground floor, the loft was his special refuge. He would retrieve the lesson plans from storage in the crawlspace and spend hours reading and writing, assisted by whatever light could filter up from the dwindling fire. He spent much time on writing, although his father had warned him that penmanship is like swordsmanship—it would be around a long time, but it wouldn't be a necessity and would most likely become a lost art.

On the evening before Philip's eighteenth birthday shortly after dinner, he and Sarah were summoned by their father for the nightly lesson. After descending the ladder, he was excited to see his father walking toward the fireplace while loading his favorite pipe. This was a hint that tonight would be special. Philip hastened over and sat on a pile of firewood. It was to be one of those rare occasions when father would stray from the usual lesson topics to fervently expound on general knowledge and offer worldly advice. Father was intrigued by the interactive relationship of the earth, sun, and moon. He would put forth personal insights, such as why the so-called sunup should more amply be referred to as earthdown. The illusion of the sun coming up is due to the earth's rotation. He noted that although the sun is much larger and farther away than the moon, they both appeared to be the same size as a shilling when viewed from Earth. He pointed out that tornadoes, volcanoes, earthquakes, geysers, waterfalls, thunderstorms, rivers, breaking waves, and the wind blowing through the trees were all natural sounds of the earth. He also taught that like moonshine and moonlight, there was also earthshine and earthlight. Sunlight reflects off the earth to dimly illuminate the moon's dark side. The moon's far or dark side exists because the rotation of the earth and moon are synchronized so we always see the same side and never see the other side.

A favorite topic was when father recalled examples of exitrants in his life. The word exitrant is a portmanteau of exit and entrance. An exitrant is when a person exits a phase in their life and enters a new phase, while totally being unaware of the change, at the time. One can only realize that the transition had occurred through hindsight. An endotrant is when one enters a situation and experiences an immediate distinct impression that there is a potential for it to evolve into an exitrant. Father also stressed the power of the Japanese belief in Kaizen, supporting an individual's ongoing practice of constant improvement ultimately for the better.

Another favored subject was William Shakespeare, whose former theatrical colleagues John Heminges and Henry Condell had meticulously compiled his comedies, histories, and tragedies together with their own recollections, in 1623. This First Folio contained thirty-six of his thirty-nine plays, eighteen of which would have been lost to oblivion. These works contained words and phrases that would become part of the English lexicon: "countless", "fashionable", "in one fell swoop", "faint hearted", "for goodness sake", "neither rhyme nor reason", and "too much of a good thing", to name a few.

He would often follow these insightful presentations with whimsical rhetorical questions, such as, "When you are searching for a lost item, why do you always find it in the very last place you look? Because once you've found the item, you don't look for it anymore!"

As Mary strolled over to join the rest of the family, she affectionately ran her hand slowly across William's shoulders. He responded with an immediate pat on her rump, accompanied by an obvious squeeze. They were a genuinely loving couple enjoying their lives together, with many fulfilling years yet to come. To Philip's amusement, he had seen Sarah blush at the sign of affection setting up what was to follow later that night. Although Sarah was nearly twenty years old, she had always been shy and quiet, but still waters run deep. She also hadn't had the opportunity to spend time with boys. Her facial features were plain and she had inherited her father's short, stocky stature, but not his confidence and high self-esteem. Philip had his mother's sharply defined proportional facial features, above average height, with lucid blue eyes and pitch-black hair. He was irrefutably handsome, and at almost eighteen years of age, already towered over his father, but his enormous respect for his father never wavered.

With the family assembled, William spoke from topic to topic with everyone contributing except Sarah, who felt that her comments were unworthy, and thus unwelcome, which was an utterly unfounded notion. The others would always try in vain in an attempt to extract Sarah from her self-imposed shell. Although father's presentation was directed to the family in general, the topics seemed more applicable to Philip, who after all, is the first-born son. This favoritism did not cause Sarah to be envious, as she accepted the mores of the time to afford the first-born son a kind of divine rite, unspoken though it may be. She loved Philip. After about two hours, William ended the session by stunning the family with an announcement.

Every fall, William would send the annual harvest down river to Williamsburg by way of a boatsman, at a negotiated fee. He would haul the tobacco by wagon, in several trips, to be loaded onto a large barge featuring a huge sail. Although the harvest was many months away, William informed his family that this year they were all going to travel to Williamsburg along with the harvest because he had to purchase some supplies and tools that he needed to select personally. He explained that he would hire a separate boat for the family's round trip. They were all understandably thrilled at father's announcement and they joyfully thanked him.

There were, in fact, two reasons for father's decision for the family trip. One he had just verbalized to his family, but the second reason was to remain unspoken for now, as it would be revealed enroute. Unbeknownst to his wife, who would surely protest, William had arranged with Mary's brother James, and his wife Emily, to leave Sarah in Williamsburg with them for a time. Of course, William planned to relent if his wife and daughter objected, but he had become increasingly alarmed at Sarah's declining mental state. He feared for her future should she remain isolated in the wild indefinitely and he wanted to provide her with an opportunity to build confidence and self-assurance. Before the family retired to bed, he made another announcement directed at Philip that he was to receive a special gift at his birthday dinner the next day. In addition to the exciting announcement about the upcoming trip, this was indeed welcome news to Philip, who had never received any presents, of much magnitude, even at Christmastime.

Chapter One

Philip's long-anticipated eighteenth birthday seemed to take an eternity to pass as he tended the field and went about his other daily chores. Finally, his mother rang the bell, announcing dinnertime. Philip raced to the cabin, washed his hands, hurried to the table, and sat down. After grace, he virtually inhaled his meal of pheasant, vegetables, and bread. The package, his present, had laid on the table throughout dinner in front of father, who seemed to eat his food at a much slower rate than usual. Although Philip was aware that the package was obviously a book, he was still incredibly anxious to discover its contents. Finally, William ever so slowly pushed his empty plate to the center of the table. With Mary and Sarah intently taking in the scene, father handed the package across to Philip saying, "Philip, I had the boatsman pick this up for me last fall, and now on your eighteenth birthday, I'm happy to give it to you and I truly feel that you will appreciate the significance of this gift."

Philip proceeded to quickly rip the paper off a very heavy and thick brown leather book and exclaimed, "A book!"

William recognized his son's obvious disappointment and realized that Philip was trying to cover up his true feelings, with feigned excitement. Lowering his voice, William said, "It's much more than a book, it's your book, specifically it's a journal. Your personal journal. Take a look inside."

Philip slowly lifted the cover and saw on the first page the inscription *To Philip Winemore Ambruster on his Eighteenth Birthday*, underneath were the words *To Thine Own Self Be True*. The rest of the pages in the journal were blank.

William stood, picked up his chair, and moved next to his son. Leaning in close, he said, "As we've discussed over the years, remember that you must hold yourself accountable for your actions, be able to live with your own conscience, and always be truthful to yourself and others. This journal will enable you to keep a record of both your accomplishments and your failures." Recognizing that Philip still wasn't comprehending his point, William continued, "Your life so far could be considered as blank as the pages in this journal. Make something of your life, never give up, and if you live a good life, you will reap your just rewards. The best way to accomplish this is to keep a log of where you've been, so you can determine where you want to go and why."

Philip's facial expression reflected that he finally understood his father's point and relayed this fact to him by earnestly saying, "Thank you, father. I understand."

William responded with a broad smile and continued, "I hope you fully grasp my advice to you this evening. Hopefully, someday you will have a son or daughter." He glanced over to Sarah, who immediately looked down at her folded hands. He continued, "And when you do, at the appropriate time, the words you enter into this journal will assist you in putting your children on the right path. The way your mother and I have tried to do with you and Sarah." William moved away from his son, stood up, clapped his hands together and said, "Enough is enough, and I've spoken enough, it's up to you now, off to bed, it's late. Good night."

"Philip, another bit of advice, if I may. In life, you cannot control most of the confrontations you experience, but you do have control of your reaction to these adverse or favorable actions toward you. The fashion in which you address and handle these encounters is a measure of your strength of character. It's difficult, but always strive to find encouragement in discouragement."

As Philip ascended the ladder to this loft, with journal in hand, his father added softly, "And one more thing, Happy Birthday. Your mother and I love you and Sarah very much. See you in the morning." William headed off to bed.

"Good night, father," replied Philip, but being too shy to express his love, he just said, "Thanks so much again for my journal," and he continued up the ladder. Upon reaching the loft, Philip reached up to the shelf for his Indian ink and quill feather while contemplating making his first entry. He sat there alone, with some light provided by dying fire below, but no words came to his mind. He gave up, but instead of placing the journal up on the shelf, he decided that the crawlspace would be more appropriate for safe keeping, along with other family valuables, already hidden below the floor. He climbed down from the loft silently, so as not to disturb his slumbering family. The trap door creaked as he lifted it, but nobody seemed to stir, so he continued down into the dark space. He blindly felt around in the closest corner and found the canvas bag he knew was there. He placed the journal in the bag and pulled the tie strings taught. He carefully, almost reverently, inserted it into an opening between two of the floor support beams imbedded in the cabin's foundation. This would be the repository for his journal and all the rest of his important belongings from now on. This gave him a good feeling inside.

He started to lift the trap door when the still of the night exploded with loud, wild, animal-like yelping. Five Shawnee Indians burst through the front door. During their uncontrolled frenzy, the solid oak table fell on top of the trap door. Although the trap door was weighed down, Philip was able to slightly push the door up to see the turmoil in the room above. He considered forcing the door but decided this would be unwise. He saw his father run in from the saltbox addition with his always-loaded flintlock musket in hand. William raised, leveled, and aimed the weapon at one of the intruders, firing a shot into his forehead and killing him instantly. The four remaining Shawnee braves were infuriated. Two of them disarmed William and secured his arms while the other two pulled Sarah and Mary from their beds, where they had been cowering in absolute terror. Screaming hysterically, they fought desperately in a failed attempt to get free from the captors.

William was powerless to help his wife and daughter, so he continued to struggle with all his strength to break free, but the two braves were much too strong.

In the darkness of the crawlspace, Philip retrieved the bag containing his journal, with the screams of his mother and sister echoing in his head, he crawled across the dirt floor in the direction of the firewood chute. Shaking uncontrollably, Philip climbed quickly up the wooden ramp, that just days earlier he had used to send down fresh firewood. He struggled to the top of the chute, pushed open the small, hinged door near the base of the chimney, and clambered out into the side yard. The cold night air jarred his emotions to a higher level and the sweat on his face seemed to freeze solid instantly. On quivering legs, Philip ran through the field carelessly smashing the young plants beneath his bare feet. He dived into the underbrush to catch his breath and get his thoughts together. He hated himself for not going back to save his family, but his instinct for survival and common sense prevailed in that moment, and he knew that any attempt would be futile. As he lay there and listened to the distant sounds of the ongoing carnage, every muscle in his body was cramped in frustrated rage.

Inside the cabin, as William was being retrained, the Shawnee holding Mary unsheathed a knife and sliced her throat from ear to ear. With Sarah's screams filling the room, he watched in horror as what appeared to be a bright red necklace flowed down his wife's white nightgown, spreading into a liquid apron of blood. Mary slumped to the floor, gurgling for air as she died, with her eyes bulging in a silent plea for William to help her. Unable to avert his eyes, he stared at his wife's lifeless body, and an uncontrollable madness boiled within. William mustered herculean strength, broke away from the Shawnees, pulled a tomahawk from the waistband of the nearest one, and jammed it into his face, practically slicing it in half. Knowing there was no chance of survival, he threw the tomahawk at the one who had slaughtered his wife, but the weapon flew aimlessly across the room. The three remaining intruders easily overpowered William, stabbing him repeatedly in an unabating assault, with a now-freed Sarah looking on. He felt the pain from the first puncture, but all the others felt like dull punches into a detached body. William died panicking over what would happen to his Sarah and frantically wondering what had happened to Philip during this gruesome attack.

Thankfully, Philip didn't witness the actual brutal murders, but the sound of the violence was enough to send him into a state of shock. Through blurred eyes, he watched the remaining Shawnees load the contraband from his home, onto the backs of two horses, who were now riderless. There was no way for him to know that one of the objects flopped across a horse's back was his sister Sarah, bound by her hands and feet. Confident they had ransacked all the blankets, supplies, and food they needed, the cabin and barn were set afire, cremating all four bodies. The Shawnees slipped away and disappeared into the thick of the woods with the overloaded horses, to rejoin their tribe.

The Shawnee tribe, from the Ohio River valley, was one of eight tribes that were allies and trading partners with the French, who were at war with the British colonists. They served as scouts and soldiers for the French during the ongoing French and Indian War. The Mohawk tribe was among the tribes that serve in this same capacity for the British colonists. Although there was some violence toward the British colonists dating back as far as 1752, in the western most region of Virginia, the official start of the war was 1754. The Ambrusters were aware of the periodic violence surrounding them for the past couple years, but they shared a false sense of security until the Shawnees shattered their world this night. The war would rage on for another seven years, ending in 1763 with the signing of the Treaty of Paris.

Philip continued to lay in his hiding place with a pillow of moss absorbing his seemingly endless tears. He didn't sleep, but he was not awake either. He was in a sad and ugly world from which he feared he would never escape. He awoke to a cloudy, dreary morning, and for the first time in Philip's memory, the birds were not singing their usual morning serenades. Only these muted songbirds, in the safety of the highest tree branches, witnessed his dumfounded exit from the cover of the bushes to make his way to his now destroyed home. He walked unsteadily back through the field and across the creek, with pointless apprehension deep down in his stomach that his father would be very angry with him for all the plants he trampled in his escape. The cabin was completely leveled, except for the original field stone chimney and the newer red brick one, both of which remained standing, as if to defy the reality of the devastation. The bodies were unretrievable underneath the charred debris and several columns of smoke rose steadily from the ruins. Philip sat and starred at the destruction until early afternoon, when he finally stood up, picked up two pieces of lightly burnt planks, found a few loose nails, and fashioned a cross using a rock for a hammer. He then pounded the cross into the ground where the front door had been. Philip's attempt at a prayer was overpowered by his growing resentment and bitterness toward God.

The rest of the day was filled with waves of grief causing unstifled sobs, until there were simply no tears left for release. He picked up the canvas bag containing his new journal, the only physical remnant of his previous life, and began his trek east away from the setting sun. He realized that, again, he was surrounded by an eerie silence, except for the hissing of the smoldering heap. Philip left the field and entered the path to an unknown future and turned to look back at what was once his home—his life. He saw a mockingbird, with white-patched wings aglow in the dusk, repeatedly taking flight straight up and immediately returning down to the wooden cross below, joyfully singing its usual evening songs, with some renditions on loan from other birds.

I am forcing myself to make this first entry to attempt to leave the past behind me and look to the future. In honor of my family, I will own today, tomorrow, and the next day, making them worthy to join the happy days gone by.

May 1756

Chapter Two

After a few hours, Philip stopped to soak his aching and bleeding bare feet in a stream flowing toward the river. He scrounged together a dinnertime snack of wild blueberries and acorns, cracked open with his teeth. Thank goodness it was a mast year for the oaks as they were producing enormous amounts of nuts. He ate half-heartedly, although he was absolutely famished. Suffering from sheer exhaustion, he dropped to the ground, leaned against a tree trunk, and drifted off into fitful shallow sleep. In this semi-conscience state, he devised a plan to travel to Williamsburg to seek out his Uncle, James Winemore. He assumed that Uncle James and Aunt Emily would take him in. He also resolved to recall as much family history as possible and enter the information into his journal. After tossing and turning, he slipped into a deep, restorative sleep. At first light, he awoke revived in body, but more discouraged in spirit than the day before. His crying jags became less frequent, but the pain of sorrow and relentless guilt nagged him constantly. He would never forgive himself for failing to, at least, try to save his family and he suffered from the resulting survivor's guilt. He resumed his journey, on an empty stomach and heavy heart, hoping to find something to eat soon.

The woods opened into a large boulder field, later to be known as the Devil's Marble Yard. Succumbing to vast loneliness, depression, and hunger, Philip climbed onto a huge boulder and screamed in desperation, at the top of his lungs, "I don't want to be alone anymore!"

From the woods behind him, floated eerie words of caution, "We won't be alone much longer mon ami if you keep shouting invitations to our heathen friends."

Philip quickly spun around, on his granite stage and surveyed the silent surroundings, but he could not locate the source of the warning. He demanded, "Who's there? Where are you?"

"Up here!" yelled an accented and annoyed voice, from a tree, in the woods that Philip had just exited.

Philip looked up into the nearby tree and saw a rough looking man sitting high up on a thick branch. "What are you doing up there?" Philip asked as he slid down the side of the boulder and approached the tree.

The tree dweller replied, "I was trying to get some sleep until you happened along trying to arouse all of God's little creatures and perhaps some big, mean-spirited ones too." The man climbed down from his perch, rope in hand, and jumped down, landing in front of Philip, who immediately retreated a few steps, not out of fear but rather to escape the terrible stench coming from the stranger. It smelled like he hadn't bathed for two months. If the truth be known, it was closer to almost four months. The man had a full beard, shoulder-length hair, and straight, white teeth that shone from his hairy face. He was dressed head to toe in buckskin and his French accent alluded to the likelihood that he was a trapper or hunter.

"What's your name and what are you doing out here?" inquired Philip, with genuine interest, having never encountered an individual anything quite like him.

"My given Christian name is Claude Devereaux, but I insist that my friends, especially my lady friends, call me Pierre. I was trapping and I'm now heading back to cash in my furs."

"It's nice to meet you, Pierre, I'm Philip."

Pierre leaned back, put his hand on his chin in mock contemplation, as to whether or not accept this young man as a friend and he continued to stare at Philip intently.

Sensing he was being scrutinized, he added, "Ambruster, Philip Ambruster" and he extended his hand.

Pierre shook his hand firmly and said, "Pleased to make your acquaintance my new, young friend, and pray to tell, what are you doing out here in the middle of nowhere?"

With this question, Philip started to choke up, but he was able to hold back the tears, much to his relief. "Indians killed my parents and my sister. They burned down our cabin and barn. I'm the only one left, so I'm headed to Williamsburg. Hopefully to live with relatives."

"I'm very sorry to hear that, Philippe. I saw the flames when I came down the river the night before last, and I knew it meant no good," Pierre said with genuine sympathy for Philip. To break the tension and change the subject, he reached into his pocket, withdrew a small sack containing some hunks of dried meat, and handed one to Philip.

"Thank you, I'm starving," he said between loud, lip-smacking chews. "This is the best beef jerky I've ever tasted."

Pierre also took a big bite and said, "It's not beef. It's either deer, squirrel, rabbit, or snake. I dry out any kind of meat I can. Believe me I'm glad to have it on cold, winter nights when food cannot be found. I think the piece you're eating is snake."

Philip wasn't sure if Pierre was joking with him or not, so he shrugged his shoulders and replied, "Snake is my favorite," he said as he continued to devour his first real meal since his birthday dinner, almost three days before.

Pierre put his hand on Philip's shoulder and guided him to sit down as he said, "You better slow down, or else your stomach will throw it back at you. That would be a waste of good grub." Pierre continued, "You are in luck my newfound friend, I'm headed for Williamsburg, and you're most welcome to accompany me. I'll enjoy having a traveling companion for a change, and you can help with the paddling."

"Paddling? Do you have a canoe?"

"But, of course," replied Pierre. "Did you think I'd be out here on foot? It's hidden down at the riverbank."

"That's wonderful. Thank you so much!" exclaimed Philip. He then asked, "Where are you from? Originally, I mean."

"Where do you think I would be from?" inquired Pierre, slightly irritated by that the question had even been set forth in the first place.

Philip immediately replied, "France."

"You are correct, but why did you ask? Allow me to give you some advice, don't ever ask a question when you already know the answer, unless you're a lawyer. It's a sign of stupidity and a waste of time to ask pointless questions." Pierre punctuated his admonishment with a sharp, steady stare.

"Sorry," responded Philip surprised at Pierre's demonstration of such abrupt anger.

"And never apologize unless you are truly at fault for something important. I can see you have a lot to learn." Pierre stood up, grabbed Philip's hand, and yanked him to his feet. "Let's be on our way. We have a long way to go."

As they headed toward the river, Philip realized that he had instantly liked Pierre, who reminded him so much of his father. A man seemingly of the wilderness, but in possession of so much wisdom and common sense. Pierre's manner of speech and knowledge conveyed that he surely had some sort of education, maybe even some formal education. He surmised that Pierre was in his late twenties or early thirties, but it was difficult to tell for sure. He was afraid to ask him lest he get another scolding. However, he did venture a statement, "I assume you've been a trapper for a long time."

Pierre smiled broadly and replied, "I fancy myself as an entrepreneur. I trap, but I also hunt, trade, and barter. I possess a good sense of character and I know when I'm being lied to, taken advantage of, or wrongfully ignored. For example, I was a scout for General Braddock about five years ago in the Pennsylvania colony. I resigned and headed south because the general and a young, inexperienced colonel, I think his name was Washington, both blatantly ignored my advice. We were ambushed after they insisted on an attempt to retake Fort Duquesne from the French. We survived, but I was lucky to get out of there with my hide."

After some consideration, Philip advanced what he believed to be a legitimate question, "Being French, why did you take sides with the English against the French?"

"Even though I was born in France some thirty-two years ago, I owe my allegiance to no country or cause. My allegiance is to myself, and that is my creed. I must tell you that the French are responsible for your family's death. They agitate the Shawnees against the British and encourage raids on innocent settlers to hasten the end of the war in their favor."

Pierre continued down to the riverbank into the shade of some large trees, whose branches bent down to the water. He removed some cut tree branches from on top of a canoe, uncovering the contents, including supplies, beaver pelts, and other small bales of animal fur. He reached down into the canoe, pulled out a pair of moccasins, and threw them over to Philip, "Here, you need these more than I do."

"Thank you," blurted Philip, with obvious relief, as he quickly slid them onto his sore and blistering feet.

"You're quite welcome my friend, and you are lucky yet a second time," he said, finishing the removal of the branches. "I would not have had room for you if I hadn't traded some pelts for this musket." As he pulled the gun from the canoe, he added, "I got the better trade for sure. I always do. Here's a paddle. You take the front."

They shoved off and glided smoothly into the current to begin their trip southeast to Williamsburg. It was Philip's first experience in a canoe or any boat. He was floating for the first time. He enjoyed the sensation immensely until his knees started to hurt from kneeling for so long, but he chose not to complain and continued paddling. The unlikely pair, an orphaned farmer boy and a seasoned French woodsman made good time the first day and were about to stop for the night. Looking for a good place to go ashore, Pierre spotted three Indian canoes pulled up onto the bank further downstream.

Using hand signals to alert Philip of the eminent danger ahead, he motioned him toward the bank where they could take cover in the low hanging foliage. "We'll wait here until later tonight, then continue past those grounded canoes and the camp," whispered Pierre. "Try to get some sleep. I'll take first watch."

Philip fell asleep in the soft comfort of the furs, and slept soundly, thankfully without his usual tormenting dreams. Pierre never woke him for the second watch, and Philip awoke after a few hours feeling refreshed, but he still had the constant mourning ache in his gut.

Pierre offered him dried meat, by saying, "This one is dog meat. Delicious. It'll put hair on your chest."

Philip replied, "Good, I like dog meat better than snake." He took a large tearing bite, as he chewed, he added, "Yes, this is a lot tastier. Do you have any dried skunk legs?"

This struck Pierre so funny that he could not refrain from laughing aloud, so he buried his face into a pack of furs and laughed until he could regain his composure. As he finally lifted his face from the pelts, he said, "You're going to be alright Mr. Philippe Ambruster. You're definitely going to do just fine," Pierre's laughing fit was more of a release of built-up tension and free-floating anxiety than a reaction to Philip's attempt at humor. Although, he did feel much better after the hysterical jag and hoped that the anxiousness that has been plaguing him of late would soon not return.

After a long, boring wait for the darkness of night, the first hint of the rising moon unfortunately showed it to be a full moon in a nearly cloudless sky, but Pierre knew this would be the case. He casually mentioned, "Every full moon has its own name, this is the Flower Moon to signify the blooming May flowers. It's also called a Blue Moon because it's the second full moon, in the same calendar month." He then rattled off all the other names, in calendar order, "Wolf, Snow, Worm, Pink, Strawberry, Buck, Sturgeon, Harvest, Hunter's, Beaver, and Cold. I consider them all my big, fat friends."

They waited until midnight, assuming the Indians would be fast asleep, to push off and paddle silently to the middle of the river and continue past the encampment. The moon was full and so brilliant that the lunar craters and mountains usually visible, were bleached out by the brightness. The sky was light blue with a single cloud glowing white. Pierre pointed to the cloud and told Philip that it appeared to be moving in the direction of the moon's position. They paddled on and stopped fifty yards upriver from the canoes and camp to wait for the cloud to hopefully drift into place. Thankfully, the cloud cooperated and crossed in front of the moon casting the dark shadow they needed to pass by undetected. As they quietly floated past the camp, the cloud continued its glide allowing reflected sunshine to reappear from the moon's surface. The ensuing light seemed brighter than before and Philip held his breath. He couldn't hear Pierre breathing either. Through some good fortune, they were not spotted from the shore. Evidently, the Shawnees didn't feel the need to post a guard on the bank, which germinated an idea in Pierre's head.

Further downriver, they pulled their canoe ashore to rejoice in their success and get some well-earned sleep. The celebration ended abruptly when Pierre looked over at his elated travel partner and proclaimed, "Philippe, we have to go back."

"What?" Philip shrieked in total amazement. "Are you out of your mind?"

"Did you see all the pelts in those canoes? I can stay in Williamsburg all next winter if we take them, and you will have additional resources to finance your future."

"No, I didn't see them. My eyes were shut the whole time and I am certainly not going back. Let's just get the hell out of here." Philip was shocked at his use of profanity, but he was frightened, and he knew any opposition to the contrary that he could muster would surely fall on deaf ears or heard but be promptly refuted by Pierre.

"Listen, Philippe," responded Pierre, with fatherly tenderness, "They are not the raiding party who killed your family, but they're from the same tribe. We can't kill them, but this is your chance to exact your revenge by relieving them of the pelts that took months of hunting and trapping to acquire."

Philip thought long and hard about the revenge aspect of Pierre's argument and relented. "Alright, I'm with you, Pierre, but I'm afraid."

"That makes two of us. The true mark of a brave man is admitting fear. Any man who would purport to not being afraid in a situation like this, is either a fool or a liar."

They returned to the canoe, boarded, and headed back upstream, with their every move illuminated by the moon and no clouds in sight. They had paddled dangerously close to the camp, when Pierre whispered, "Let's get out here and go the rest of the way in the water."

"I can't do that," Philip desperately hissed back, "I can't swim."

"Either can I," Pierre replied, "but it's not deep if we stay close to the bank. Just keep your eyes peeled for snakes, especially Cottonmouths. It's the world's only semiaquatic viper and it can deliver painfully, fatal bites. But I forgot, you like snakes. Let's get moving."

After securing the canoe on the bank, not bothering to cover it, they removed their shoes and shirts and slid into the water. Without saying a word, Pierre broke off a nearby reed, pinched off both ends, inserted it into his mouth, and went underwater for a full minute. After this demonstration on how to hide submerged, Philip broke off his own thick reed, and they waded waist-deep in the direction of the camp. The canoes came into view, with obviously no guards present. The setting moon would soon be accompanied by a rising sun. Philip's heightened fear and elevated adrenaline increased his sensory perception levels making the water feel ice cold. The sound of the rustling leaves above seemed deafening. As they inched closer to the canoes on their stomachs and the water yielded to the shoreline, they heard foot falls coming in their direction. Simultaneously, they scooted back to deeper water, put the hollow reeds into their mouths, rolled over, and disappeared beneath the surface. While underwater, Philip's already exaggerated hearing was magnified tenfold. He could hear the Indian leaning on the rocking canoe, rummaging for something. Pierre perceived the same activity and continued to take steady, slow breaths through his reed. After the movements and sounds subsided, Pierre cautiously removed his knife from the sheath and quietly rose through the surface. He caught a glimpse of their unwelcomed guest walking back up the path with something in his hand.

So as not to panic Philip, Pierre just waited for him to surface on his own, but he positioned himself closer, so he could reassure him as soon as he emerged. Sensing it was safe, Philip surfaced and was relieved to see Pierre, with his index finger over his lips.

Pierre said, "I assume he found what he was looking for, and of course it was in the last place he looked."

Philip glanced at Pierre and saw a flash of his father's face, he furrowed his brow, and replied, "Of course."

In unison, they struggled to free the heavy canoes from the shoreline. When all three canoes floated free, they pushed them further out to catch the slow-moving current. Together with three unmanned crafts, two floating heads drifted downstream to safety. Upon reaching their canoe, Pierre strapped the two Indian canoes together and directed Philip to tie the third one to their canoe. In the glow of the approaching sunrise, the set of canoes, containing two very relieved and tired passengers, quickly headed downriver as if in a race to beat the sun to the horizon.

The silence was broken when Pierre suggested, "Let's travel all day without stopping. Once the Shawnees realize what happened, they'll run beside the river until they drop."

Philip laughed in whole-hearted agreement until Pierre cautioned him about the noise, although they were clearly out of earshot of their victims, there could be others around.

In the early evening, they pulled the canoes ashore, found a suitable clearing, and built a fire. Lacking the luxury of fresh meat, they had another meal of dried meat. Their supply was almost depleted since Pierre's personal portions were being consumed twice as fast now by two hungry souls. Although Pierre had not slept at all the night before, and Philip had just a little sleep, they lazed and gazed into the fire. There was little conversation as they were both in reflective moods. They silently stared into the hypnotic flames and deep into the scarlet caverns within the burning logs. Philip watched as the moths, attracted to the fire light, would flutter around the fringes, until they would come too close and fall into the flames. He shared his observation with Pierre.

Pierre asserted, "Things aren't always as they seem. Those bugs see only the beauty of the firelight hiding the inherent danger that is always looming within. Many situations in life are like this. Always, keep your guard up and expect the unexpected." He jumped up and said, "We better get some sleep and get an early start. I'd like to arrive in Williamsburg the day after tomorrow as early as possible. And we're almost totally out of food."

"We're that close?" asked a shocked Philip as he followed Pierre to a nearby Oak tree. Pierre nodded his head in confirmation and started to climb the tree with two lengths of rope.

"Why do you sleep in trees?" queried Philip, as he was looking around for a place on the ground to settle down for the night.

Pierre explained, "I would like to tell you that it's the way of the woods or for protection from the savages and wild animals, but quite simply, I hate bugs, any kind of bug. I've tried sleeping on the ground, and if there are bugs present or not, my imagination conjures them up and I itch all night."

"Do you mind if I join you?" asked Philip. "I don't care for bugs either or any other nocturnal critters."

"Please do. I'd be insulted if you didn't," laughed Pierre.

They climbed high into the tree and Pierre demonstrated the art of wedging into the fork of a branch. Philip accomplished the procedure easily, so Pierre began to tie him to the forked branch with a rope.

"What the hell are you doing?" protested Philip. "I'll be fine. I'm jammed in here."

"The knack of tree sleeping is the ability to stay securely nested in your perch after you're asleep," advised Pierre.

"I don't want to be tied up and I won't be," Philip said forcefully, as he removed the rope from his leg, dropping it to the ground.

"Suit yourself, but if you break your neck in the middle of the night that's your problem, not mine," promised Pierre, tying himself securely to his branch.

The conversation ended without another word, and they were both asleep within minutes. A few hours later, Philip crashed loudly to the ground. Fortunately, because he was unconscious and his body was limp when he hit the ground, no bones were broken, but he sustained some deep scratches on his face and arms. He climbed back up the tree, snugged himself into position, and didn't complain when Pierre knotted him into place. The next morning, they both agreed that although they could make it to Williamsburg by sunset, it would be prudent to camp one last night and arrive at their destination in the daylight. After eating the last of the jerky for breakfast, they pushed off toward the final leg of their trip. After two hours of paddling and no lunch, Pierre suddenly hollered over to Philip, "Let's stop here."

When they hit shore, Pierre grabbed his prized musket, bolted from his canoe, and ran into the woods, yelling back, "Secure the canoes and make a fire!" Shortly thereafter, Philip heard the loud crackle of gunfire. Momentarily, Pierre reappeared from the woods dragging a small dead deer that he spotted from the canoe feeding in a field. Pierre expertly butchered the animal, and an hour later, they feasted on a dinner of fresh venison. They retired early in anticipation of the journey's end, without further discussion because they were both in reflective moods and wanted to contemplate their own personal thoughts.

Philip's excitement to see Williamsburg was cast in the shadow of ambivalence because the guilt of not having saved his family had not lessened and he knew it never would. He also felt guilty that only he had lived to make the trip that his father had promised the whole family. Why him? Why did he survive? Was it luck? Was it a message? What would his Aunt Emily and Uncle James think of his survival? Would they take him in?

Pierre appeared to be asleep in his snug crux, but he was staring out into the starry sky with his own conflicted feelings nagging him as the trip neared its end. It had been nice having a companion on the last days of his annual sojourn into the wilderness, but more so, he had acquired a real liking for this lonesome, tormented young man. Philip reminded Pierre of himself years before when he had willingly left his family to work passage on a ship for parts unknown in search of fame, adventure, and perhaps fortune. Pierre had begun his quest with the same uncertainty and innate courage that Philip seemed to possess. No doubt, he will never see Philip again after he unites with his family. Why was this prospect so hard for him to face? He surmised that it was the father and son relationship they had chanced into. These thoughts unburied old emotions that plagued him from time to time. His stomach churned at the realization that he was missing out by not having a wife and children. He went from one experience to another without any commitments or responsibilities. The older he got, the more wasteful and pointless his life seemed to have become. With the prospect in his head that maybe next year he would settle down, his mind yielded to sleep. In reality, he knew he would never change. At dawn, after a breakfast of leftover venison, they set out, in a speechless rush, to bring their adventure to its end and separately begin another.

I thank God in heaven that a French trapper "Pierre" Claude Devereaux has invited me to join him for the rest of his trip. I'm convinced I could not complete it on my own. My initial shock of my family's death had evolved into guilt for not having saved them, which depressed and angered me. I hope my adventures with Pierre will lead to some kind of acceptance. Pierre exudes a happy positive nature; however, I can't help but feel he is mired in a swamp of regret, loneliness, and depression of his own.

May 1756

Chapter Three

Pierre and Philip with the canoes filled with furs and pelts ready for market, rounded a bend in the river and civilization quickly came into view. Basically, it was just one large building with a sign that read Trading Post. The commotion caused by the men working at the post was quite shocking to the newly arriving travelers who had become accustomed to the silence and tranquility of the river.

After coming ashore, Pierre shouted, "Philippe, keep an eye out, and I'll go tend to our business." He turned and walked resolutely toward the Post to begin the bartering process. After a short while, Philip spotted Pierre walking back accompanied by the tallest, fattest man Philip had ever seen. After introductions, the big man, justifiably known as Bear, began to sort through the goods by throwing them into separate piles on the ground. After making calculations in his head, Bear withdrew some paper from his pocket, wrote something down with a charcoal stick, and shared it with Pierre. He agreed, "That would be most acceptable. What can you offer me for the canoes? Keeping in mind that they are authentic Shawnee."

Bear inspected the canoes, wrote down a number, and showed it to Pierre, who again said, "Yes, that too is most acceptable. I'll be back after noon to collect payment. In the meantime, would you please assist my young friend here."

After Philip inquired as to where he could find the Winemore family home, Bear replied, "I haven't been into Williamsburg for a longtime and I'm totally unfamiliar with its citizens." He added, "My brother, Jonathon Hopkins, is the blacksmith and he can answer all your questions about the residents. Just walk up that road over there and keep going until you hear the song of the anvil."

Pierre said, "You go along Philippe, and I'll meet you there later after I finish our business and tend to some other personal matters." Philip nodded and headed toward the road leading to Williamsburg, with his satchel in hand. It was a pleasant morning, and Philip enjoying his hike, picked up the pace and listened for the song of the anvil. The town came into view and it was an astonishing sight. The magnificence of the governor's palace was absolutely overwhelming. It was the tallest building he had ever seen and the brickwork was a masterpiece, with large windows gleaming in the sunlight. His attention was diverted to the steady beat of a hammer on wrought iron, so he hurried on. The sound became louder as he turned a corner to see a substantial stable and a white clapboard house surrounded by various colored rose bushes. When he entered the stable, the pounding ceased and the man wielding the hammer asked, "What brings you in here young man?"

Philip replied, "Your brother suggested that I check with you to find out where my family's house is located, their name is Winemore."

"I can definitely direct you to the Winemore house, but the family itself moved up to Boston about three months ago," informed Mr. Hopkins.

On hearing this news, Philip grew weak in the knees and light in the head. In no way had he ever imagined that his Aunt Emily and Uncle James wouldn't be here after all of this. Philip could not have known that the Winemores had sent word to his parents explaining that they were now unable to care for Sarah as planned. The message had mysteriously never made it to the Ambrusters.

Seeing his reaction, Mr. Hopkins suggested that Philip take a seat and he offered him a ladle of water from a large barrel. Philip gulped down the water and asked himself aloud, "What am I to do? Where am I to go?"

"I may be able to assist you with that," offered Mr. Hopkins. "I need help here in my shop. I can teach you the trade if you're interested. The pay would be minimal, but you would get room and board. Room would be that stall over there and board would be two meals a day with my wife Helen and me in our home yonder."

Without a moment of hesitation, Philip gushed, "I'll take it and with much appreciation to you and Mrs. Hopkins for your generous and timely offer, thank you."

It was close to dinner time when Pierre entered the stable to find Philip deep in a conversation with

Mr. Hopkins. Philip looked at Pierre in pure disbelief as he was clean-shaven and his long hair was trimmed and pulled back into a stylish ponytail. He was wearing shiny, black leather boots, tight beige pants, a blue velvet waistcoat with a crisp white ruffled shirt, and lastly, he sported a very beautiful woman on his right arm.

"My God, Philippe, you look like you've seen a ghost," Pierre declared as he affectionately patted his friend's gloved hand.

Philip tried to sputter a reply as to why he was so surprised at Pierre's new look but gave up the attempt. He explained the news of his family's departure and his new working and living arrangement with Mr. Hopkins. This was indeed welcome news for Pierre who had made his own plans that afternoon, which certainly had not included his former traveling cohort. Pierre pulled Philip to the side, and as he slipped a heavy bag of coins into his hand. He cautioned, "Here's your share of our proceeds. Tell no one of it and hide it well."

Pierre told Philip that he and his lady friend were off to dine at Raleigh Tavern. Philip started for the house to meet Mrs. Hopkins, but he spun around and ran back to Pierre and his lady friend. "Before we part ways, I'd like to ask you a question that I've been pondering for some time. You told me that your given name is Claude, but you go by Pierre. Why?"

With a slight smirk, he replied, "Claude is from the Latin word claudus, meaning crippled or lame." With that Pierre turned and walked away feigning a pronounced limp as he shouted over his shoulder, "Au revoir, mon ami until we meet again." With a pang of sadness, because Philip doubted they would ever meet again, he ran to catch up with Mr. Hopkins, who was entering the house. An early supper was being set on the table, and Mrs. Hopkins added another place setting since they had company. After the meal, he borrowed a quill and some ink and returned to the stable to make his periodic journal entry.

Philip stayed with the Hopkins for close to a year around his nineteenth birthday. Jonathan and Helen were like parents to him, filling a huge void in his life, and he loved learning the art of blacksmithing. He was well over six feet tall and now weighed more than two hundred pounds of solid muscle, owing to the laborious nature of the work. His bright blue eyes belied the gaze of a dreamer, but on closer inspection, they portrayed the true nature of this young man's personality—determination and intestinal fortitude. He was happy to have been invited to stay in the extra bedroom after the first month, but there was a growing restlessness within. He longed to travel the world, starting with a pilgrimage to Boston to locate Uncle Thomas and Aunt Elizabeth Ambruster, and Uncle James and Emily Winemore. Philip shared his intentions with the Hopkins one night during dinner. They remained calm and listened emotionlessly to Philip's plan, but inside they were both deeply crushed. They had both grown to love this young man, having never had children of their own. By way of an unspoken visual conversation, through eye contact alone, a talent known only to couples together for many years, they agreed to withhold their immense disappointment. They verbally extended their total understanding, agreement, and support of Philip's proposal to seek out his family and they wished him well.

I am grateful beyond all measure to Jonathan and Helen Hopkins for restoring in me the gift of abiding family love that I had unfortunately lost. This natural love is so often taken for granted by some, or worse, totally ignored by others.

September 1757

Chapter Four

Taking Mr. Hopkins' advice, Philip hitched a ride to the port city of Norfolk with his satchel containing the journal, his money, a few clothes, and some food prepared by Mrs. Hopkins. On his arrival in Norfolk, as luck would have it, Philip secured accommodations on the first ship he boarded. The TIDEWATER was slated to depart for Boston in two days, but its captain, Horace Brackett, insisted on taking the passage money in advance to guarantee Philip a private cabin. Upon the denial of his request to stay aboard for the next two nights, he set off to find the inn that Captain Brackett recommended. They demanded an advance payment as well, but the room was clean, and the charge included breakfast. After a modestly priced dinner, Philip retired to bed, slept soundly, and arose early with excitement and optimistic anticipation for his upcoming adventure of a lifetime.

The next morning, Philip began to explore Norfolk. He ended up down at the docks where he decided to take another look at the TIDEWATER to ensure it was seaworthy, not that he was qualified to make such a determination. When he reached the dock that he had just visited the day before, the ship was gone. The unscrupulous Captain Horace Brackett had accepted Philip's money and set sail two days early leaving him stranded. Philip would come to learn that Brackett had a reputation for cheating unsuspecting travelers. He didn't do it for the money. He did it as a joke and for fodder to brag and laugh about over his tumbler of rum.

Philip still had money for passage so he found the harbor master's office to inquire about other ships that would be sailing for Boston. The harbor master, a small man with a huge bulbous nose, disavowed any knowledge regarding Captain Brackett's shenanigans, but he highly recommended Captain Henry Gramond, whose ship the CHARMING NANCY was scheduled for departure the next day. After getting directions to a remote area of the port, he spotted the ship, approached it, and figured the man barking orders to the crew was the captain.

"Excuse me, Captain Gramond, may I have a word with you?" He shouted over the loudness of the constant activity on the wharf.

Looking down from the deck, Captain Gramond replied, "Come aboard and state your business."

Philip relayed the entire story, which was no surprise to the captain, who replied, "Low life people like that are a scourge to those of us who have a love for ships, the sea, and the numerous ports-of-call we call home."

Philip paid the charge for the supposedly last so-called cabin onboard but rejected an offer to stay that night because he had a pre-paid room with breakfast, and he inherently trusted that Captain Gramond would not depart without him. He left assuring the captain that he would return early the next day in time to catch the outgoing tide.

After a sporadic night's sleep, he got up before the usual prepared breakfast, so he quietly snatched some fruit from a bowl, put it into his bag, and set off quickly for the dock. Captain Gramond, who was a serious, medium sized man, stood at the top of the gang plank and welcomed him aboard, with a hearty handshake.

"We push off in twenty minutes. In the meantime, I'll have my first mate Limey show you to your quarters," he said while signaling the first mate to come hither. Limey was a small, wiry fellow, who loved to eat limes, a fruit that English sailors ingest at sea to prevent scurvy. A good thing. Bananas brought bad luck if brought aboard. A bad thing.

His quarters turned out to be a windowless room, about the size of his stable stall back in Williamsburg, located down in the airless bowels of the ship. It appeared to be a former storage area, with no furniture and two scratchy woolen blankets sewn together and filled with straw for a mattress, but no bedframe. The floor was a malarial swamp of standing, dank water harboring infested mosquitoes, as evidenced by the infected bumps Philip would soon have on his body. As Limey began to leave, Philip strongly considered going with him to complain, but he decided to just settle in. Within ten minutes he could feel the ship moving and he was thrilled to be headed to the open Atlantic for his long-awaited trip north to Boston.

The voyage was a disaster from the start. The first night, the ship was engulfed in a raging thunderstorm with high seas that tossed the CHARMING NANCY relentlessly. If he had a bed, he surely would have been thrown from it, and if he had any furniture, he certainly would have been thrown into it. Adding to his misery, he suffered continuous seasickness and spent the trip self-quarantined in his cabin. At least the captain regularly sent down two meals a day, but he could barely tolerate the food. At last, the torturous trip seemed to be ending because one evening, he sensed that the ship was in calmer waters. Later that same night, he became delirious with severe sweating, a very high fever, and uncontrollable shivers.

Even though Philip was very ill with what would later be confirmed to be a case of malaria, he became aware that the ship was now motionless. In a total stupor, he packed up his belongings and struggled up to the deck, where he headed directly to the gangplank. He stumbled down the plank, staggered up a street away from the ship, and walked a few blocks. Philip finally collapsed in the small alleyway between the back wall of a building and a small hill.

A patron reported the situation to the proprietor of the Man Full of Trouble Tavern, Joseph McCorkle, who along with his daughter, Abbey, went out back to investigate. McCorkle was a fat, scruffy, unkept widower, with a cantankerous disposition. He resembled the image painted on the sign out front, featuring a pirate, with a monkey on his shoulder. Abbey, the barmaid, was pretty, with light brown eyes and matching brown, short hair. She was the spitting image of her mother, who had died giving birth to her after a very extremely complicated and fatal pregnancy.

"This man is drunk on his arse," proclaimed McCorkle as he rolled the listless body over with his foot, giving it an extra kick for good measure, to prove his point.

"No, he's not father," argued Abbey noticing the stranger was burning up with fever. She pleaded, "We must help this poor man or he will surely die if left unattended."

After an unyielding confrontation with Abbey, McCorkle called for his son Paul, who helped him get Philip into the attic room. Paul had bright red hair and green eyes inherited from his maternal grandfather, who had always bragged were the rarest of all human eye colors. Meanwhile, Abbey secured Philip's things and placed them into the tavern's storage room. She placed the bag in a closet for safekeeping next to an ornate box containing a pair of dueling pistols. The weapons were always loaded and ready if need be.

"Fetch the doctor Abbey," ordered McCorkle, as he told Paul to pull off Philip's boots before dragging him into bed, so as not to dirty the sheetless mattress. "And mark my words, this man will pay for the room and the doctor's bill, one way or another."

Ignoring her father's rant, Abbey rushed from the tavern, past the family townhouse up the street to the doctor's stately home on Delancey Street.

Philip laid there in a fever induced delirium, oblivious to the fact that the CHARMING NANCY had pulled into port for emergency repair of storm damage, but the port was not in Boston. He was in a bed, inside a tavern, in the colony of Pennsylvania, in the city of Philadelphia.

Abbey returned with Dr. Wistar, who examined the unconscious man and diagnosed him with malaria having already assumed that, after hearing Abbey's description of the man's symptoms. He reached into his bag and retrieved two separate bottles containing the only two compounds that were known to treat the illness, even though the malaria parasite had to run its natural course in the long run. Considering the man's apparent age and overall fitness, the doctor made a favorable prognosis and predicted a full recovery.

Dr. Wistar assigned Philip's treatment to Abbey, "You must get two tablespoons of each medicine into him twice a day until it's used up. That will take exactly four days." Under the watchful eye of the doctor, Abbey fed the first dose of the two medicines to Philip, who swallowed the syrup on reflex. The doctor, McCorkle, and Paul exited the room, leaving Abbey alone with her new patient. She stayed with him night and day, sleeping on the floor, only leaving to tend to her own nourishment and refreshment. Although she didn't even know the man's name, and they had never exchanged words, Abbey fell more and more in love with this stranger with each passing day. On the morning of the fourth day, she woke, stood up, and crossed the room to prepare the first daily dose. She had determined early on that the easiest way to administer the medicine was to mix the two compounds together in a cup. Turning away from the dry sink, she was so startled to see the man sitting up staring at her that she gasped and nearly spilled the full tin cup onto the floor. She barely saved the concoction.

In a weak, dry voice, he asked, "Who are you and where am I?"

She answered, "I'm Abigail McCorkle and you're in our tavern. We found you four days ago in the alley out-back unconscious, feverish, and totally incoherent. The doctor says you have malaria and I've been tending to you ever since."

"Well, thank you for your attention, Abigail, and if I may again intrude into your kind nature, may I have a drink of water and something to eat?" He perceived that his dramatic manner of speech in his request sounded like something Pierre would say.

She crossed the room and gave the cup to Philip, who took it and drank it down for the first time on his own. She re-filled the tin cup with water, and said, "They call me Abbey. I'll go fix you some eggs and coffee. I'll also bring some hot water and soap so you can clean-up, even though I've been taking care of that too." After this unintended, blunt confession, she blushed, and Philip grinned.

Halfway to the door, Abbey stopped, spun around, and asked, "Who are you and where are you from?"

"I'm Philip Ambruster from Williamsburg Virginia and I'm here in Boston to locate and unite with my family. Do you know the Ambruster or the Winemore families?"

With a confused expression on her face, she replied, "First of all Mr. Ambruster, you're not in Boston, you are in Philadelphia. Secondly, I know of neither family here." On hearing this, Philip was so shocked that he could make no verbal response at all and his mind scrambled to make sense of this unfolding predicament.

After a few days, Philip was a hundred percent better but not yet a hundred percent well. He rationalized that his mistake of leaving the ship after an unscheduled stop in Philadelphia was an error he could have made with a clear head, so he forgave himself and moved on. His drive for Boston and family was compromised now that he was fending for himself precluding the need to seek out the support of his family. As he pondered these thoughts, the CHARMING NANCY was sailing south down the Delaware River toward the mouth of the Delaware Bay flowing into the Atlantic Ocean to continue her trip north to Boston. A perplexed Captain Gramond stood on the deck wondering what had possibly happened to the young man, who had disappeared from his ship in the middle of the night. He shrugged his shoulders, shook his head, and went below to the galley for a quick lunch before returning to the bridge.

Guided by their own objectives and personal interests, Abbey and Paul successfully convinced their father to employ Philip. Of course, he had to move out of the attic to free up the room for an occasional paying guest. He would bunk in the first-floor storage room where his possessions were already stowed. Abbey needed him to stay because she loved him and was sure she could earn his love in return. Paul was happy to have someone else perform the unsavory duties that come with running a tavern, including all the shit jobs. He also welcomed more free time so he could increase his hours at his other job as a waiter, at the larger and more prestigious City Tavern at South Second Street. Paul particularly enjoyed serving at private parties catered by City Tavern in the local neighborhood known as Society Hill. Named after the Free Society of Traders, Society Hill was comprised of merchants and landowners, with offices on a hill overlooking Dock Creek. City Tavern is directly across the street from the Slate Roof House, formerly the city home of the founder of the province of Pennsylvania William Penn. The site would eventually be named Welcome Park, after the ship WELCOME that had brought Penn to America in 1682.

I was never so sick in my life, but I now realize that it takes such a serious illness for one to fully appreciate how wonderful it feels to be healthy, physically fit, and mentally alert.

July 1759

Chapter Five

After a few months, Philip had adapted to the routine of the tavern, and he had grown to enjoy everyday life in Philadelphia. With his health fully recovered, he regained his strength and felt even stronger than before his illness. Walking the cobblestone streets, he was oblivious to the side glances made in his direction by many interested young women. The work was not rewarding, but he embraced being part of a family and quickly accepted Abbey as a well-needed replacement for his sister Sarah. He knew that Abbey's affections for him were more than brotherly love, and of course, he would never take advantage of her frequent flirtatious advances toward him. On those occasions, he would take evasive measures and laugh it off.

One evening, when he returned from a break, he entered the rear door and heard a very loud disturbance in the main room. He immediately recognized Captain Brackett's loud, slurred voice and grabbed the dueling pistols from the shelf in the storage room. He quickly entered the room and saw that Captain Brackett had Abbey on his lap. She was ineffectively struggling to break free from his groping hands, sloppy kisses, and rank breath. His first mate Spike, nicknamed for a hideous scar on his left cheek inflicted years ago by an instrument of the same name, was holding a large sharp knife to McCorkle's neck. He was bleeding as profusely as the curse words flowing from his drooling mouth.

With both pistols aimed at Brackett and Spike, Philip demanded, "Let her go Brackett and drop the knife or I'll blow both your heads off." Brackett complied by standing up and roughly throwing Abbey to the floor and then stomping on her while she was down. Spike defiantly threw his knife across the room imbedding it in the doorframe of the rear entrance. Philip handed the pistols to McCorkle, who took careful aim at the two scoundrels, hoping for any excuse to let the hammers drop.

Philip crossed the room in one fluid motion and grabbed the bag of coins sitting on the table in front of the Brackett. "I'll take repossession of the money I paid you, plus interest, for the passage you did not provide and never intended to provide."

Although the old man eagerly had the captain in his sights, Brackett still grabbed a large pewter stein and smashed it across Philip's jaw. The ornate engraving on the heavy mug left a bleeding imprint on his face. Brackett then hurled the stein at Abbey, striking her on the collarbone and drenching her blouse with the remaining warm, stinking rum.

Infuriated by this blatant act of pure hatred, cruelty, and absolute meanness, Philip swiftly pocketed the money and smashed his left fist into Brackett's jaw in an uppercutting motion. When Brackett's head flopped back down, he struck his nose hard with his right-hand fist, resulting in a loud cracking sound as his nose broke and gushed with blood. With all his might, he punched him in the gut causing him to double over, just as a customer was entering the front door. Philip spun him around and kicked him in the backside, out the open door, onto the sidewalk. He headed for Spike, who scurried like a wharf rat toward the backdoor, retrieved his knife, and ran away without looking back. Philip returned to the front door as Brackett struggled to get up. Philip shouted, "Don't you ever set foot in this neighborhood again. If you do, you won't have the option of getting up."

Brackett, wiping blood off his face snarled in a primal growl, "You're a dead man." Philip slammed the door closed and turned around to the applause of the patrons, who had witnessed the entire incident. Philip, having never laid a hand on another man in anger, just barely managed to stop his hands from shaking. He quickly concluded that Brackett deserved the beating, but he also deduced that he had just created a very daunting enemy.

Later that night, Philip was dozing when he sensed someone slipping into his darkened room. He was relieved, but startled, to see it was Abbey, who proceeded to drop her dress to the floor and climb into his bed. She pressed her lips against his ear and whispered, "I want to thank you for what you did tonight." Feeling her warm breath on his neck, Philip clambered out of the bed and ordered her to get dressed and leave at once. He immediately regretted his harshness.

In a softer voice, he added, "Abbey, I love you like a sister, but it could never be more than that. I'm sorry if I've misled you." She was crushed because until this moment, she truly believed she had a chance to win over his affection and that he was just being coy. Without another word, and with her clothes in hand, she left his room in tears. Philip felt terrible, but at least, and at last, the status of their relationship was settled. After close to an hour of re-living the evening's events over and over in his mind, he finally fell asleep.

The next morning Abbey silently toiled with her chores while ignoring Philip, who was failing in his attempt to begin a conversation. The tension was broken by McCorkle's entrance into the room announcing, "Philip, my boy, thank you again for your assistance last night. I want to increase your responsibilities here at the tavern, but there is no increase in pay, mind you. First, I want you to accompany Paul to the bank to make a deposit and meet the people there."

It was a beautiful day as Philip and Paul strode down the walk at a good clip. They entered the office shortly after opening. Just when Philip walked in, he came to a total stop and his mouth dropped open in absolute awe. Across the room, standing with an older gentleman, was the most beautiful girl he had ever seen. She had long blonde hair and magnificently big blue eyes. Seeing the stupefied state Philip was frozen in, Paul smacked him across the back of his shoulder saying, "What's wrong with you? Keep moving!" He followed Philip's line of sight to the subject of his trance and added, "Forget it. That's Julia Clayburn, of one of the wealthiest families in Philadelphia. She is with her father and see that gentleman working over there at that desk, that's her fiancé Robert Morris! As a matter of fact, it's not official yet. It's more of an understanding between the Clayburn and Morris families, but from what I hear, it's a sure thing."

"How do you know all of this Paul?" he asked without attempting to hide his annoyance.

"My catering jobs. The first thing you learn is how to eavesdrop. It's easy. When you're in a uniform, the guests treat you like a piece of furniture and they spill their guts. You must keep your head down, your eyes peeled, and your ears open. Now, come on, let's make the deposit and get out."

Philip reluctantly followed Paul to the teller to make the deposit and be introduced. He then coerced Paul into lingering outside to await the departure of Julia and her father. As they exited, Philip heard Mr. Clayburn instruct the driver to proceed to City Tavern.

Despite his better judgment because he feared his father's wrath should he be late returning from the errand, Paul still agreed to take Philip to the Clayburn residence on Pine Street. It was located in the opposite direction from the Man Full of Trouble Tavern. Philip was understandably impressed by the Clayburn mansion, which unlike many of the houses in Philadelphia, stood separate from the neighboring townhouses. It had pure white marble steps leading to a massive door protecting a prestigious entry hall. They stood across the street surveying the house when the Clayburn carriage came around the corner into view and continued down the cobblestone street. They slipped behind a nearby stinky ginkgo tree as the carriage came to a halt at the bottom of the front steps. The now lone passenger, Julia, exited the rig instructing the driver, "Please take the carriage around back. We won't need it until dinner, thank you, Jasper."

Philip saw his chance, so he stepped out from behind the tree and strode across the street. Paul quickly retreated homeward. As she ascended the steps, Philip shouted, "Excuse me Miss Clayburn. May I have a word with you?"

Julia looked at him questioningly and asked, "Do I know you sir?"

"That's what I would like to speak to you about. My name is Philip Ambruster", he offered, as he took her hand and attempted to kiss it, which seemed at the time the proper thing to do.

Julia yanked her hand back asserting, "I beg your pardon, sir. You are being very improper, and I want you to leave me alone and go away!"

Upon hearing the disturbance outside, Collins, the Clayburn's butler, opened the front door and inquired, "Is there anything wrong Miss Julia?"

She began to answer "No", but then playfully continued, "Why yes, this gentleman is making rude and improper gestures and I would like him to leave the premises."

"That's not so. I just wanted to talk with you. I meant you no harm," Philip countered taking another step up. Collins rushed down to confront him while motioning for Julia to go inside. As Collins insisted that Philip leave now or face the consequences, Julia was intently peering out the side glass window framing the front door, with a gleeful smile and a twinkle in her eye. She thought this young man was surely unlike anyone she had ever met.

Philip reluctantly agreed to leave saying, "Please tell Miss Clayburn that I'll speak with her another day when she isn't so busy."

"Yes, I shall relay your message sir, good day," replied Collins turning to go inside.

Julia walked up the winding staircase toward her bedroom with the uncontrollable smile still on her face and a gleam still in her eyes, as she said aloud to herself, "Yes, Mr. Ambruster, you do that, you do just that."

"What did you say dear?" asked her mother coming down the steps to inquire about the loud confrontation at the front door.

"Nothing mother. I was just talking to myself."

On seeing Collins, Mrs. Clayburn asked, "What was all that noise outside?"

Not wanting to alarm her, he said "Nothing really, Ma'am. Just a young suiter for Miss Julia who needed to be discouraged. He is gone and I don't believe he will return."

"I should hope not," she replied returning back up the staircase to pry more details from Julia, who again refused to provide any further information. She entered her room to take a nap and dreamt of the young man she had chastised. It was a good dream.

The next day, Philip described to Paul the details of his conversation with Julia on her front steps. Paul angerly replied, "You're going to end up behind bars!

And where will that leave me? Besides stuck with all the shit jobs again!"

"That reminds me, I need a break. I'll be back in about twenty minutes." Philip left and headed in the general direction of Pine Street. Minutes later, much to his pure delight, he spotted Julia walking towards him on the same side of the street with her alleged fiancé Robert Morris. He approached them and boldly took Julia's hand from the crook of Robert's arm and gallantly kissed it on her incredibly soft knuckles. "Julia, my dear, how nice it is to see you again so soon. I'm sorry I didn't have the time to converse with you at length yesterday. Perhaps, I can find the time to stop by again early next week, at your convenience of course."

Visibly flustered by this second chance encounter, she nervously replied, "No that won't be necessary." Regaining her composure, she added, "In fact Mr. Ambruster, I strongly believe it's improper of you to even make such a ridiculous suggestion considering I don't know you and I haven't the slightest inclination to get to know you. Please let us pass."

Robert finally interceded, "My good, man. I do believe Miss Clayburn doesn't wish to associate with the likes of you, and I must insist that you take your leave immediately."

Amused by the situation, Philip graciously bowed and sarcastically agreed, "You are obviously correct my good man. I shan't bother Miss Clayburn again and I beg her forgiveness." The three parted company and continued in their original opposite directions. Philip had advanced less than ten paces when he ventured a peek at the departing couple. He was exhilarated to see that Julia had turned her head to look back at him in the same instant. Their eyes met and locked in place causing them both to smile instinctively. It was then and there that he knew beyond any doubt that she was his true love, and they were undeniably destined to be together. He hurried back to the tavern to tell Paul about this encounter. He also wanted his own ears to hear what had just happened.

Back at the tavern, Paul was so taken with this very promising development, although it was just a matter of two requited smiles, that he launched a plan to assist Philip in further pursuit of their budding relationship. With a sly grin, he calmly mentioned, "There is a party at the Powel house this Saturday evening that City Tavern is catering and I am scheduled to work. I know that the Clayburns will be in attendance, but unfortunately Julia's fiancé will also be there. I want you to go in my stead. You can wear my uniform. It'll be snug, but it will do. Just tell my manager that I'm sick and you're filling in for me." Philip was encouraged by the fortunate offer and cheerfully thanked Paul and promised to re-pay the favor someday. Saturday evening could not come fast enough.

I have met the woman of my dreams. Although she is betrothed to another, I vow to win her heart. I simply cannot imagine my life without her. I truly love Julia with all my heart, soul, and being. I know I always will.

August 1759

Chapter Six

Philip arrived at the Powel's home near Third and Spruce Street early to scope it out and found a beautiful townhouse with formal gardens in the back surrounded by a six-foot-tall brick wall. There was a small, square brick building at the back of the yard, which was being put to good use as the meeting place for the caterer's crew. The others wore the same uniform that Philip was sporting complete with formal tails on elaborate waste coats, but theirs fit perfectly.

Philip entered the rear gate, approached the man who was addressing the staff, and introduced himself as the temporary replacement for Paul McCorkle, who was much too ill to work. The manager stepped back and studied Philip from head to toe, noticing the ill-fitting clothing but choosing to ignore the tightness of the outfit and asked, "Do you have experience serving and caring for the type of important guests we are expecting tonight?"

Opting for honesty, Philip answered, "No I don't, but I've been working at the Man Full of Trouble Tavern and I know how to keep customers happy."

Not wanting to be left short-staffed, the manager said, "I don't want to trust you with the food and beverages, so I'll keep you to the side and place you later. For now, go inside and position yourself next the fireplace in the drawing room. Don't say a word and speak only if you're spoken to. Now go!"

He crossed the expanse of the backyard, cutting around formal gardens, and entered the house. Not knowing what or where the drawing room was, he headed for the first fireplace he spotted and took up his position just when some guests were entering the front door. From his vantage point, he could see two men, who repeatedly referred to each other by their surnames, step across the threshold in a loud, heated debate, and they came directly to his room. Totally ignoring Philip, Messrs. Kuhn and Butler continued their political argument, and it was clear they would never come to an agreement. Interestingly, in the future, the Kuhn mansion on Chestnut Street would become home to the republican Union League of Philadelphia, before moving to a new brick clubhouse on South Broad Street. The Butler mansion, at Thirteenth and Walnut Street, was destined to become The Philadelphia Club, a democratic stronghold, into which one had to be born.

Listening to them arguing, he noticed the arrival of Mr. and Mrs. Clayburn and Julia, but there was no sign of Robert. The din of the ongoing debate faded and his heart skipped a beat as he watched Julia glide into the ballroom, with her parents. Shortly thereafter, Robert entered the house and joined the Clayburns. Philip noticed that they were not a happy group. This further convinced him that a Morris-Clayburn match must be discouraged and intercepted at all costs. They just didn't look right together at all.

The evening continued uneventfully, and Philip was never transferred from his original post, so he decided to make something happen. He spotted a man, who was obviously part of the house staff. He confronted the man in the hall saying, "Excuse me sir, a guest has requested that I deliver a message to Julia Clayburn, but I don't know who she is. Would you please point her out to me or be kind enough to deliver it for me?"

Eyeing the catering uniform, the house servant surmised that it was a legitimate request, "I will personally deliver the message to Miss Clayburn. What is it?"

Philip relayed the contrived message, "A gentleman has asked her to please meet him as soon as possible in the backyard, beyond the gardens, at the pear tree near the rear gate."

Just when Robert and Mr. Clayburn retired to another section of the house with some other gentlemen, and Mrs. Clayburn joined a group of friends, the servant delivered the message to Julia, who was now alone.

With a rising tickling sensation in her stomach and a building hopefulness that the invitation might be from Philip, she asked, "Do you know this gentleman?"

"No, but I will be happy to accompany you if you wish, Miss Clayburn," he offered.

"That won't be necessary but thank you."

Julia swept out through the garden doors with a feeling of anticipation unlike she had ever experienced and rushed into the darkness toward the back wall. She saw the pear tree and slowed her pace so as not to appear too anxious, but no one seemed to be there. After looking around, Julia shrugged her shoulders and started to head back to the party. From the side of the small building, a soft low voice startled her for a moment saying, "Leaving so soon?"

"Oh, it's you again," she complained, as she turned and started to walk back to the house.

"No wait, please come back," Philip begged as he ran after her. He caught up with her and led her by the hand back into the shadows, so as not to be seen from the main house.

Still holding her hand, he desperately said, "Just a minute, please Julia. I truly want to apologize for my past rude behavior. It's just, well, I've never met anyone like you before. It's more than your beauty and the way you carry yourself. It's that everything about you is so fresh and unique. From the first moment I saw you, I knew I had to meet you, and I'm sorry for approaching you in such a brash fashion. But I can't help myself," he whispered with a quiver in his voice.

With this, they both realized that he was now gently holding both of her hands and they looked down together at their coupled fingers. Slowly, their mutual gaze moved from their intertwined hands up to their faces and they locked eyes without saying another word. Philip bent down and lightly put his lips on her mouth. He pulled back, looked deeply into Julia's eyes, and happily sensed that she had similar feelings for him. With renewed vigor, he kissed her again, more aggressively and strongly embraced her. Suddenly, the music from the quartet that had been drifting through the gardens, came to an end and the sound of the men returning to the ballroom could be heard.

"I must go back," Julia softly said to Philip, whose life had just changed dramatically, with a future path that has been altered forever.

"Julia, I love you," gushed Philip in a voice with a hoarseness and sincerity he had never known existed in himself before. He couldn't believe he had expressed the words out loud, let alone to Julia.

She moved closer, and gazing into his eyes with a confused expression said, "I don't know how this could have happened, but I believe I love you too. I need time to sort things out, but I know my feelings for you are true and that will not change. I see now that these feelings began on the steps when we first met, but I refused to admit it to myself until now."

She turned on her heel and ran back to the house, stopped at the doors, turned around facing into the pitch-black yard and mouthed "I love you." Julia blew a kiss to Philip, who she knew was still watching her from the shadows, and she continued inside with a flip of her hair and a snap of her dress.

Philip left the premises, forgoing his pay. He didn't need the money in the wake of the evening's incredible turn of events and he returned home to share the great news with Paul.

The next day, Julia conveyed the sudden development regarding Philip to her parents, who had never seen her so happy. They were flabbergasted but remarkably understanding. Her mother admitted that she knew there was more to the story of the incident on the front steps. She also shared that lately, she was becoming more and more disenchanted with Mr. Morris, and Mr. Clayburn wholeheartedly agreed. His primary concern about Philip was his apparent station in life without a bountiful career to support the needs of his daughter. He intended to meet with the young man to ascertain whether he qualified or had the ability to earn a qualification for a position in the family's thriving import-export business. The next day, Julia informed her fiancée Robert that their relationship was over. He appeared much relieved. Shortly thereafter, Robert at age thirty-five, married Mary White, age twenty, and they raised their seven children at his home on Front Street. He would never give Julia another thought.

Philip proposed to Julia within one week, on the front steps of her home, and she accepted in a heartbeat. They spent the following days together every chance they could and enjoyed picnicking in a clearing within a wooded area that would be the site of the new State House. They were entertained by the constant goings on down the street at the Potter's Field.

Julia's father was out of town on business and Philip was to meet with him on his return regarding Philip's possible entry into the family business. In the meantime, their love for each other grew by leaps and bounds as they began to really know and love one another more and more with each passing day. Their common likes and dislikes were uncanny.

Mr. Clayburn returned to Philadelphia the next Monday. Julia told Philip that he was to meet with her father that Wednesday, as he needed a day to recover from the trip. He most likely required more time to prepare for the interview of his future son-in-law. Philip had a remarkably good night's sleep, waking Wednesday morning clear headed and with a very positive attitude. He walked briskly up Dock Street toward the Clayburn offices near the Customs House.

He was internally rehearsing possible answers to probable questions he may receive and did not notice a covered wagon that had quickly come up behind him and abruptly stopped. Three large men grabbed him, knocked him over the head with a club, and threw him into the back of the wagon where he was bound, gagged, and carted away.

I'm ready and anxious to begin a new future in the Clayburn family business, but I am also wondering if I'm cutting myself short by not exploring other professional paths.

September 1759

Chapter Seven

Philip regained consciousness on a filthy floor with an excruciating headache pulsating from a crusty wound. He groggily recognized the sway, sounds, and vibrations typical of a ship at sea. His wrists were tied at the waist with another length of rope extending over to an iron ring embedded in one of the rotting wooden ribs within the hull next to him. He recalled his abduction, but he had no clue as to how long ago that had been. Without a doubt, he immediately knew that he was on Brackett's ship TIDEWATER. Accepting that he was in dire straits, he made a conscious effort to rest, recuperate, and await Brackett's next move. That came two hours later when Spike kicked him in the head. With assistance from another crewman, they cut Philip loose from the rusty ring, smashed him into and around a bulkhead, and roughly dragged him stumbling up onto the deck. Although it was the middle of the night, most of the crew silently surrounded him, curious as to what hideous fate their ruthless and demented captain had in mind for this poor soul.

"My, my isn't this a pleasant surprise? It's so thoughtful of you to come for a visit. I guarantee you will not enjoy any minute of your brief stay, and I guarantee it will be brief," taunted Brackett. With no emotion in his voice, he said, "You made a fatal mistake that night in Philadelphia. You should have finished me off because now I'm going to finish you off."

Philip began to speak, but Brackett smacked the side of his head with the broadside of his sword while he ordered, "You men over there, grab that gangplank and slide it over the railing." It took three sailors to lift the heavy lumber, slide it across the railing, and place the other end on top of a big stack of overstuffed burlap bags containing worn-out sails. Brackett then ordered the men to secure it and stand on that end of the plan while he commanded other men to lift Philip onto the plank. They forced him to stand up and walk to the end by poking him in his back with their swords until they could no longer reach him. Brackett ordered him to jump off the plank, which of course, he refused to do. Without Philip having said anything to the deranged captain, Brackett's lips formed a sick, wicked grimace. He turned his attention to the men standing on the end of the plank and yelled, "Jump off now or you'll be next!" They immediately complied.

The plank seesawed over the railing, plunging Philip into the blackened water below. The TIDEWATER continued the easterly cruise toward her European destination, with the crew members slowly and quietly returning to their stations or bunks. Except for Spike, who laughed as he dutifully shadowed his captain below decks. Brackett was anxious to have his nightly overdose of cheap rum and bedtime snack of overly buttered, stale, and tasteless muffins.

Philip and the board splashed into the water, and fortunately, they bobbed up together through the surface at the same point of entry. Even with his hands still tightly bound, he managed to slide his arms over the end of the plank and shimmy down so that he could wrap his legs around the other end and lock his ankles together. It was a long, frightening night hugging that timber for dear life, but he was able to remain in position and not flip over. His imagination ran wild, producing frightening thoughts and terrifying images of various monstrous sea creatures that were surely going to devour him. He forced himself to focus on positive thoughts, including possible rescue scenarios. After uncountable hours floating on the calm sea, with a very slight breeze, the sky began to brighten in the east. It was comforting to have a sense of direction and time again. With the rising sun came another welcome sight. A bird, without webbed feet, landed directly in front of his face, and seemingly, its blinking, beady eyes were intently studying him. The bird's exhaustion was evident by an open beak exposing a panting, pink tongue. It surely had flown out from dry land that must be reasonably close. While Philip was being entertained by the first flying fish he had ever seen, he noticed a complete rainbow arching from end to end attached to the horizon that was encircling him. Although he was in the middle of the ocean, he had an overpowering perception of being on the sphere of planet Earth. Philip literally drifted off and passed out into a deep sleep indicative of a likely concussion. He awoke in the midafternoon to the best rescue scenario yet. A distant mirage foggily took the shape of an approaching ship. He tightly closed his eyes to clear the thoughts inside his damaged skull. A short time later, he ventured another look, assuming that he would see an empty ocean, but the mirage was closer and had become more realistic than before. Although he had never given in to his fearful imaginings and maintained his optimistic assumption of ultimate survival, he was now experiencing pure exuberance. He was sure that it was not a hallucination and that an actual vessel was definitely heading directly toward him and closing in fast.

Meanwhile, on the approaching ship MIRALTO, the ship owner's son, Alexander Newbold, had spotted the floating debris and directed the captain, Thomas Tarrant, to change course. Noticing the distinct course adjustment, Alexander's father, James, came from below to join him on deck as they closed in on the debris that now clearly included the body of a man. At the first sign of movement, Captain Tarrant ordered a safety line with a loop on the end to be thrown into the water. Although the ship was still moving, Philip was able to disengage from the plank and hold onto the thick rope as crewmen hoisted him from what would have been a watery grave. Now onboard, he unsuccessfully attempted to stand up, while his feathered companion effortlessly flew up to the highest lookout post nicknamed the crow's nest. Suffering from sun exposure and dehydration, Philip was given water, carefully carried below to a bunk, and the rope was finally cut from his aching, swollen wrists.

The next morning, he was flustered by the memories of the last few days that rushed into his brain, but he felt remarkedly revived and cogent. Momentarily, Alexander appeared with water, fruit, and a friendly greeting, "Good morning. I'm Alexander Newbold, call me Alex. My father and I are merchants and import-export representatives. I'll get my father while you're eating, and you can tell us both your story." Alex had brown hair and matching brown eyes, with almost identical physical body dimensions and weight as Philip. They could pass for brothers. After ten minutes, Alex reappeared with his father, and they sat on stools next to the bunk.

"My name is Philip Ambruster and I had a run in with a Captain Horace Brackett." Upon hearing the name, the father and son exchanged knowing glances. Philip continued, "A couple of days after the confrontation with Brackett, his men knocked me out, delivered me to him, and he threw me into the ocean from his ship to inflict his revenge against me."

Mr. Newbold said, "We're aware of Captain Brackett's reputation, but this goes beyond the pale. This is a clear case of attempted murder for which he will have to be held accountable. I'll go with you to the authorities when we arrive in Philadelphia."

"Philadelphia!" proclaimed Philip. "This ship is heading to Philadelphia?" He had not even considered inquiring as to the ship's home port or destination, as his brain was still not functioning at full capacity.

"Why yes, our company is based in Philadelphia. I hope that will give you a good start to your travel home."

"It's perfect. I live and work in Philadelphia, and I neglected to mention that's where Brackett kidnapped me."

"Ah, another charge to be pressed when we get home." retorted Mr. Newbold. "Rest up Philip. Come on deck to stretch your legs when you feel you can handle it."

After a few hours, Philip felt recovered enough to venture topside. He spotted Alex on the other side of the ship, waved, and proceeded towards him. Suddenly, with no warning at all, a rogue wave slammed into and over the starboard side picking up Alex and carrying him across the deck over the portside railing. A typical rogue wave is at least twice the size of the surrounding waves. The large and powerful wave is the result of two waves converging from opposite directions resulting from two separate storms at sea. Philip fortunately had a strong grip on a nearby post as the ship listed to the left and then immediately righted itself, in the now placid ocean. Having seen the coiled rope that had just been used to retrieve him hours before, he lunged for it, put the loop around his waist and jumped into the sea. Luckily, he spotted Alex thrashing to stay afloat. He wrapped his arms around him as the ship continued forward pulling the rope taught, which kept them both above the surface. Some crew members, who had seen Alex being washed overboard, began pulling on the rope that was luckily fastened to a railing. It took four men to hoist the two back onto the deck, owing to their combined weight being at least four hundred pounds. Now safely aboard, Alex turned to Philip and said, "Thank God you know how to swim! I would have been a goner."

Philip laughed as he replied, "Swim? I can't swim, but I'm certainly becoming very accomplished with rope." Alex joined Philip in nervous laughter as they both took a second to recover from the near-death incident.

That evening Mr. Newbold, Alex, and Philip gathered for dinner. Mr. Newbold was tall, slender, and possessed an engaging personality. He had premature pure white hair, appeared calm and relaxed, but Philip could tell he had something on his mind.

Mr. Newbold spoke first, "Philip, I want to sincerely thank you for saving my son's life today. Your fast actions and bravery prevented what would have been an unspeakable horror for Alex's mother and me."

"Mr. Newbold," Philip interjected. "It was not a heroic act on my part. I was afraid and shaking the entire time with fear."

"Philip, it's not brave if you're not scared and fortune favors the brave. On another matter, you had said you live and work in Philadelphia. Exactly what do you do and where do you live?"

"It's quite a long story, but I live and work at the Man Full of Trouble Tavern."

"Oh, with old man McCorkle. How's that working out for you?" teased Mr. Newbold good naturedly.

"It's a temporary arrangement. I was going to interview at my fiancée's family business before the untimely interruption with Brackett. I was en route to meet with Mr. Clayburn to discuss the possibility of obtaining an entry-level position with his firm."

Stunned by this revelation, Mr. Newbold said "I know the family well, and Julia is a wonderful young lady. I've watched her grow up. You will make a handsome couple. I'm sure you'll produce a wonderful family, and I believe that is what life is all about. May I put forth another possible option for your consideration?"

"Of course, sir," replied Philip.

"Family businesses can be very complicated, especially if you're an in-law and not what one would call blood, as in blood relative. Don't get me wrong, it depends on the family, the nature of the business, and the other individuals involved, but I don't want you to set yourself up for disappointment, failure, or both."

"And your suggestion, Mr. Newbold?"

"Clayburn and I are in similar import-export merchant enterprises. We're competitors, but we're also allies when the need arises, and it has in the past, with favorable results. I like and respect him. If you proceed with your current plan, it will most likely work out, but as I said it has its risks. Only my son knows this trip is my last official act with our company. I'm retiring to spend more time with my wife and to pursue other interests. Alex is taking the helm so to speak, but we've been quietly looking for someone to assist him. I believe that person is you and these recent events were fateful, and you are the man for the job. I realize this offer is based on very little history between us, but I truly feel that greatness comes from small beginnings. The plain truth is that Alex helped save your life and you saved his. I consider that connection to be the perfect foundation for a winning partnership. In other words, Philip, it was meant to be." Mr. Newbold continued, "The bottom line is that I'm offering you the job to partner with Alexander after I leave. Do you accept?"

Philip looked Mr. Newbold dead in the eyes, then looked over at Alex, who winked, he returned his intent stare to Mr. Newbold, and said in a firm, clear voice, "Yes, I accept, thank you."

"Splendid," exulted Mr. Newbold and all three men stood up, shook hands, and sat back down to a now celebratory dinner. It was a good night.

The final leg of the voyage was spent formulating a detailed business plan. Father and son wholeheartedly began educating their new protégé as to the subtle details and nuisances of the import-export business. They also concluded that Philip would vacate the tavern and temporarily move into the Newbold home at Fourth and Locust Streets. One of the new endeavors that Newbold intended to pursue was real estate. He had a friend who was moving from his Philadelphia townhouse to his country estate, and he had contracted Mr. Newbold to sell his property. He proposed to Philip that he would front the money for the purchase against future earnings. Philip wholeheartedly agreed to the proposal. He alone was making some very important life decisions, but he was confident that if Julia were present, she would endorse them and support him. Though painful and traumatic, the premeditated attack and kidnapping over a week ago, now defined itself to Philip to be an exitrant considering the subsequent occurrences that had now transpired.

The MIRALTO unceremoniously arrived in Philadelphia, and as soon as the gangplank hit the wharf,

Captain Tarrant sent a runner to the Clayburn home to inform them of Philip's ordeal and let them know he would be there shortly in person.

After docking, news reached the crew that the TIDEWATER was destroyed in a storm with all hands lost. The shipwreck had been identified by its nameplate floating in the water with other rotten sections of the ship and contents, including the bloated burlap bags. The ship was prone to destruction and was torn to pieces owing to years of blatant neglect, habitual non-maintenance, and irreparable abuse. Known only to the powers that be, the offending storm had been the contributing source of a wave that combined with another to become the rogue wave that had swashed Alex overboard.

In clothes borrowed from Alex, Philip noticed a small bird fly from the crow's nest as he left the ship and headed up Dock Street on his way to the Clayburn residence. He was met halfway there by Julia, who was drenched in her own tears of joy. The two hugged, kissed, laughed, and cried together as they walked to her home, where he relayed to the stunned family and servants the details of his assault, battery, and abduction. As he spoke, he too could hardly believe the particulars of his night floating in the ocean, being saved from certain death, and his role in saving his new-found friend, and now partner, Alex. The final part of the story regarding his new occupation, temporary residence with the Newbolds, and pending home purchase was of considerable interest to Mr. Clayburn. He concurred with arrangement, offered a few suggestions and seemed to take on an air of contentment. Julia was hearing the story for a second time because she had heard the details on their walk. She became more and more amazed that Philip had been subjected to this abuse and survived. The servants were excused, so Philip, Julia, and her parents could plan the wedding, to be held at Christ Church, in a fortnight.

Brackett had made four miscalculations that fateful night. He tied my hands in front of me, provided flotation, deposited me into a busy shipping lane, and the water was seasonably warm preventing the onset of deadly hypothermia.

October 1759

Chapter Eight

Philip and Julia were ecstatically enjoying their first dance as husband and wife, and their first dance ever, in the center of the ballroom to soothing orchestral music. They were encircled by their watchful guests, many of whom were members of Philadelphia's high society. Julia had never looked more gorgeous with her radiant blue eyes locked onto Philip's. He was enthralled by how spectacular she looked this evening, and he lovingly memorized every facial line defining her beauty. Her body embraced in his arms was soft, yet firm and extremely sensual, as they seemed to float around the crowded room. He would never forget this fantastic day.

As the music began to fade, they slowed their pace. Philip saw Julia's gaze drift to the right as her focus averted away from his eyes. She was alarmed by something happening over his shoulder. On pure reflexive impulse, Julia spun their coupled bodies around, exchanging their positions. Philip immediately saw the source of her angst. Standing at the edge of the dance floor, Abbey had lifted both of her shaking arms from a large, black shawl, and in her hands were the dueling pistols from the tavern.

A shot had already been fired and it had been aimed directly at Philip's back, but now the .45 caliber lead ball crushed into Julia's spine. Some of the guests screamed and panicked. Philip and Julia fell to the polished floor, now marred by a growing pool of bright red blood. While still holding his now deceased wife, a second shot was fired, and he expected a ball to rip into his body, but that didn't happen. He looked up to see Abbey's head exploding from a self-inflicted shot to her left temple, with a large exit wound gaping on the other side of her head. Her blood, bone fragments, and brain matter were splattered on those nearby. Grasping the harsh reality that Julia was dead, and that she would never be with him again, Philip screamed at the top of his lungs and wept uncontrollably. He would be inconsolable for months and he would never, ever, be happy again as long as he, and he alone, shall live. There will be no children, no grandchildren, and no growing old together.

Alex burst into Philip's bedroom during the outburst shouting, "Philip, Philip, wake up! You're having a dream! Wake up!" He shook Philip violently and slapped his face hard.

Philip sat straight up in bed, with a pillow now soaked in sweat and tears. An incredible feeling of relief expanded throughout his mind, body, and soul. He began to understand that the nightmare he had just experienced was, in fact, a real nightmare. As his emotions settled and his breathing returned to normal, he swore to himself never to share this unspeakable dream with Julia or anyone else. Although it was forever indelibly etched into his memory.

Later that day, the wedding was held at Christ Church on High Street. Julia's wedding gown was no less than breathtaking and Philip's formal attire fit him absolutely perfect. Reverend Bitzer officiated over the service and he kept it brief, as requested by the couple. The reception was considered the event of the year, so far, with everyone having an enjoyable time. Philip's contribution to the guest list had been the McCorkle family. Mr. McCorkle was his usual miserable self. Abbey looked beautiful in a new formal dress, without a shawl, and even Paul looked presentable. Alex, meeting Abbey for the first time, was immediately attracted to her and they spent the entire afternoon together into the night. After a whirlwind courtship that lasted but two months, they were to marry, raise four sons, and enjoy a long, happy life. Abbey's position at the tavern was filled by her friend Marion Engle, who would eventually marry Paul, but they would remain childless. Which was fine with them.

The newlyweds had purchased the furnished townhouse in the seven-hundred block of Spruce Street the week before the wedding through Mr. Newbold. The former owner, Nicholas Biddle, was settling in full-time at his summer country estate Andalusia, on the Gold Coast of the Delaware River, in lower Bucks County. The couple happily chose to honeymoon in their own home. The contents of the house included one of the first marble clawfoot bathtubs in America, and decades later, it would eventually be relocated to the backyard garden and put to good use as a flower planter.

In their comfortable abode, they witnessed Philadelphia's transition into a sublime city. Their alley was named Orange Street, like so many streets being named after trees, but it was later changed to Manning Street. The Potter's Field, a burial ground for revolutionary soldiers, prisoners, yellow fever victims, and the homeless, became Northeast Square. It was later renamed Washington Square taking its place with the other four city squares—Franklin, Logan, Rittenhouse, and Penn.

Life is good, maybe too good. Although I would never mention it to Julia, I cannot help but notice that the good life is most definitely adding some poundage onto her figure.

February 1760

Chapter Nine

Six months later, on August 6th, 1760, Nathan Clayburn Ambruster was born in the master bedroom on the second floor overlooking the back garden, which was in full bloom, especially the large, vivid, yellow rosebush. Although he was barred from the birthing room, Philip heard all the agitation, with several moans and a few screams. He felt and was indeed powerless to help. He was delighted with the midwife Anna for obviously doing such a professional job. After all, she had come very highly recommended and was in high demand.

Philip's primary concern was Julia's condition in the aftermath of what he had just blindly witnessed from the adjacent room. He inquired, "Anna, how's Julia doing? I was very upset hearing her discomfort, but relieved by your calm, persistent assurances. Oh, I almost forgot to ask. Is it a boy or a girl?"

"A healthy baby boy," replied Anna.

"Mrs. Ambruster is doing fine sir. We had some rough moments, but that is to be expected. After he was finally freed of the entangling umbilical cord and afterbirth, your son quickly nestled in her arms on her chest. Both patients are bonding nicely."

"I do have one worry Anna. I didn't hear the baby cry. I thought all babies cried at birth to get air into their lungs and begin their self-sustained life outside of the womb."

"I can understand your concern, and I'm truly impressed at your observation. Most fathers are so caught up in the moment they wouldn't notice. Yes, a cry-free birth is rare, and crying at birth is essential to the process and offers a huge benefit to the newborn's respiratory system. I paid particular attention to your son's heartbeats and breathing. Both are normal."

Still troubled, Philip continued, "How many cases like this have you had?"

"None. In all my years, this is the first one, but as I said, he is doing just fine, and I fully expect him to naturally gain strength, adjust to his surroundings, and flourish."

Nathan was a quiet and serious baby, with only an occasional giggle, and he became an even quieter and more serious toddler, with no bouts of laughter at all. Philip and Julia loved him immensely, even more so when the doctor informed them that Julia could bear no more children. He had become a lonely, and now only child, but the loneliness was his choice as he routinely rejected all opportunities to have playmates and later, to make friends. Friendship to most people is considered to be a basic human need, but not for Nathan. In a few years, he insisted on being schooled at home by tutors. Julia and Philip agreed to this demand without argument, knowing any other approach would be futile. So, he embarked into a solitary life void of any significant relationships, friends, or casual acquaintances. How sad.

Philip was more disturbed by Nathan's odd personality than Julia appeared to be. He just didn't seem to be a blend of their traits. It was as if Nathan was a flawed combination of random genes from distant ancestors, both fraternal and maternal. Philip had hoped they would enjoy interactive experiences resulting in a loving father-son relationship. Though disappointed, he acknowledged that his quest for a bonded coexistence with his son could never come to fruition because the requisite foundation simply did not exist. Nathan's attitude toward his father was one of pure inattentiveness. Ironically, it was this flawed trait that, after a final deathbed encounter with his father, would initiate a series of nondescript incidents. Over many decades, they would conclude with a chance discovery that would define and document Philip Winemore Ambruster's legacy for all time.

The first ten years of Nathan's life would see Philadelphia become the commercial and cultural center of colonial American life, as well as the center of revolutionary thought and activity. King George III ruled over England and imposed control over one and a half million colonists living in America. King George's hold over the colonies inspired Ethan Allen to build an ironworks and a blast furnace in 1762. They would eventually be used to produce cannons for the American cause. The next year would see the end of the French and Indian War. The Treaty of Paris forced Canada to give England all the North American territory east of the Mississippi River. It also forbade the colonists from settling lands beyond the Appalachians.

In 1764, Great Britain levied heavy taxes on the American colonies to pay for the war that had lasted years. Next, the British Parliament passed the Stamp Act, imposing a tax on newspapers, legal documents, and pamphlets. Even playing cards were required to bear an official stamp. Steep taxes were imposed on tea, paper, glass, and paint, infuriating the colonists, who began to increase their resistance. This prompted the British to sail into Boston Harbor in 1768 as a show of strength. The decade ended with the Boston Massacre on March 5, 1770, occurring five months before Nathan's tenth birthday. The so-called Boston Massacre in America was known in Great Britain as the Incident on King Street. Nine British soldiers killed five people when they fired into a crowd of four to five hundred people who were demonstrating against recent unpopular Parliamentary legislation. Paul Revere and Samuel Adams labeled the event a massacre to rile up support for their patriotic cause.

Over the next five years, there seemed to be a major conflict every year. Starting with the Battle of Alamance in North Carolina followed by the Burning of the Gaspee, where Rhode Island colonists burned a British ship that had run aground near Providence. The Boston Tea Party featured colonists who boarded English ships in the Boston Harbor and threw the cargoes of tea overboard. This action was in protest to the imposition of a tax on tea by a Parliament, in which the colonists had no representation. In 1774, the first Continental Congress in Philadelphia resolved that an attack on any one colony would be considered an attack on all the colonies. In 1775, British soldiers were ordered to Lexington to arrest the rebel leaders and seize their weapons. The rag-tag militia, led by Captain John Parker, a former British officer, received a warning overnight about the troop movement by Paul Revere. They still did not stand a chance against the world's strongest army. The Battles of Lexington and Concord, the shot heard around the world, were the first military engagements of the American Revolutionary War. The Battle of Bunker Hill, during the siege of Boston, marked the first stage of the war. Although it was a tactical victory for the British, it was a rude awakening for them as they sustained more casualties than the Americans. The Battle of Bunker Hill, actually taking place on nearby Breed's Hill, had indisputably illustrated that an inexperienced militia could stand up to regular British army troops in battle.

During this period, Nathan continued his studies at home and proved himself to be brilliant. Aside from paying close attention to his tutors, he was aloof to those around him, including his parents who had grown to tolerate his cold treatment towards them. Although he was attentive to his various teachers over the years, he hadn't established any meaningful relationships, except for one. The final tutor, Tressa, who lived a few blocks from his home, left a lasting impression on Nathan. She was by far his favorite and he was captivated by her. Tressa was a natural beauty with long curly hair, inquisitive eyes, and a devil-may-care attitude. She was well-read, well-spoken, and well-built. A true Renaissance woman, Tressa took pride in expertly educating her pupils. She inspired and encouraged Nathan to consider the practice of law and he did just that in 1776, at the age of sixteen, shortly before independence was declared.

Nathan began reading the law in a prominent firm started by Andrew Hamilton, who is credited with the distinction of being the inspiration for the complimentary term "Philadelphia Lawyer." Hamilton had successfully defended a New York newspaper publisher John Peter Zenge, who was accused of libel. Although Hamilton expertly and cleverly won the case, the "Philadelphia Lawyer" designation had more of a geographical basis. No local lawyer in New York wanted to risk their reputation by taking on the very unpopular case, so Mr. Zenge was forced to look to Philadelphia for representation.

I've put my thoughts and feelings about Nathan down on paper with the full knowledge, or dare I say assumption, that he will read them someday. Perhaps he will reconsider how he chooses to experience his one chance at life. Though late, I pray that a change of course on his part will lead to a much-needed positive change in his persona and enable him to finally enjoy those around him and bring him happiness. Parents always want what's best for their children.

June 1776

Chapter Ten

During the sixteen years leading up to the Declaration of Independence in 1776, Philip and Alex grew their business into an enterprise that others were hard-pressed to rival. The company had yielded immense financial rewards and their friendship strengthened greatly over time. They both had the same business sense and never fought, but they did have many vigorous debates that always ended in an amicable compromise. Philip and Julia's intense love for each other multiplied with every passing year along with their strong respect for each other. They also possessed a gift for engaging in heated discussions, with friendly banter, also concluding in mutually acceptable resolutions. Meanwhile, Nathan continued living at home and relegated himself to the isolation on the third floor when he wasn't at his law office.

Late in the afternoon on Friday December 21st, Julia and Philip were decorating their Christmas tree while enjoying delicious Madeira wine and aged cheese, when a loud knock echoed down the entry hall from the front door. Philip placed his glass on the table, went to the door, opened it, and his mouth dropped wide open as did his eyes, in total surprise.

"Pierre, I can't believe it. What are you doing here?", asked Philip incredulously.

"Well, mon ami, aren't you going to invite your old friend in or do I have to stand out here and freeze?" jested Pierre, with that large, toothy grin only he could muster.

"Of course, of course, sorry, come in. Meet my wife Julia", he said as he escorted Pierre into the room where she had just placed the star atop the tree.

Hearing the French accent coming from the foyer, Julia greeted him by name while offering her hand, "Pierre, I'm so pleased to finally meet you after all these years, but I feel as if I already know you with all I've heard from Philip."

"Merci. It's indeed a delight to meet you and visit your beautiful home. Obviously, you and Philippe have certainly made a wonderful life together and I'm very happy for you. I can't help but feel a tad envious."

Philip poured his long-lost friend some Madeira, which he downed in one gulp and extended the glass for a seemingly well-needed re-fill. They conversed for close to an hour, sharing stories and details of their lives since they had parted ways twenty years ago. It was eerie the way they instantly fused back together as if they had never separated. The conversation yielded to a comfortable silence and came to an end. It was time to return to the present.

"So, Pierre, what brings you here after such a long time?", Philip asked, most definitely not already knowing the answer.

"I need your help Philippe. My assistant fell and broke his leg yesterday down at the docks, so I find myself in your fair city where I don't know anybody I can trust to help me with an errand. I am not able to share the details with you until we are on the road tomorrow morning, should you agree to accompany me. I assure you this errand will greatly benefit the American cause and you'll be back home by Monday evening, right in time for Christmas."

"I'm taken aback, Pierre. I'm thirty-eight years old now, and although I'm in good health, I'm not sure if I could handle the rigors of such an important errand, or let's say mission, at this stage in my life. It's also the height of the Christmas season, and I have quite a few business responsibilities that need to be tended to with my partner."

"I'm fifty-two and have more aches and pains than I care to admit, but this mission, as you so succinctly label it, is of the utmost importance. If we stick to the plan, there is minimal risk, and when we triumph, the outcome will be something you can be proud of for the rest of your life. Philippe, I see the life you have made for you and your family, and I would never ask you to jeopardize it if I wasn't so confident that you'll return safely. We've already proved in the past that we can work well together, resulting in positive outcomes. I'm sorry for such a sudden intrusion, but it is unavoidable. I'll leave for a while to give you two a chance to discuss your decision in private."

"No Pierre don't leave", insisted Julia. "What we need to discuss can be done with you present. Turning back toward Philip she continued, "I strongly believe that this matter is more crucial than we can imagine, and I assume you feel likewise. If you want to participate, you have my full support. That Pierre would come here to request your help makes me feel you should assist him regardless of the possible risks. I think you should agree to help him."

"Thank you, Julia." He then directed his complete attention toward Pierre and said, "I'm in." The men shook hands and Julia put her hand on top covering their clasped hands, to seal the deal.

The next morning when it was still dark, Pierre pulled up out front on Spruce Street in a wagon, jumped down, and rapped on the door, which Philip opened immediately, dressed and ready to go.

"I see I'm too late", said Pierre. "I intended to arrive before you got dressed." He handed Philip a big bag containing old boots and dirty, stinking clothing. "Put these on."

"These rags smell horrible", complained Philip.

"It makes them more authentic for the roles we're playing for the next couple of days. You look like you're going to a desk job."

"Maybe I should be", mumbled Philip. After changing his clothes, he hugged and kissed Julia goodbye.

"I love you", she said with tears forming.

"I love you more", he replied, as he hugged her again and walked down the steps, pausing for a moment, wondering where Nathan was. From the top of the staircase, Nathan covertly listened to the entire emotional farewell and then withdrew back into his bedroom.

The wagon was filled to the brim with farming supplies including a small plow. The load was tightly covered with a tarp and secured by several ropes. As the horses picked up their pace heading north to Bucks County, Pierre explained that the most pressing problem the patriots were continually facing was the lack of gunpowder. Only ten percent of their supply was produced domestically, with ninety percent coming from the French Colonies in the West Indies. He informed Philip that they are posing as salesmen, who are delivering these goods to their customers. He went on to admit that, in fact, they were transporting fifty barrels of gunpowder hidden under a false bottom in the wagon. He held back the more crucial details, but he did let Philip know that their destination was a farm close to where the Continental Army was encamped.

Pierre explained, "One horse could pull this rig, but one is a spare in case the other one gets killed or injured. This applies to your role too. If something happens to me, it is imperative that you complete the trip. When you get to Bucks County anyone can give you directions to the Thompson-Neely twin farmhouse."

"Let's hope and pray that nothing happens to you or one of the horses", smiled Philip, hiding the shock and surprise he felt on hearing the magnitude of their mission. "What's our timeframe?"

"We could arrive tonight, but I rather hold up for the night and start fresh in the morning. I've arranged to spend the night at Joseph Galloway's estate, Trevose and Growden Mansion, which was inherited from his wife's family. Galloway is a notorious Loyalist. He and his wife are on an extended trip to England. My friend John Carpenter is the estate manager and he is letting us use the barn and one of the outbuildings overnight. He also manages to keep a watchful eye on Galloway, his loyalist friends, and visitors. One regular guest is Benjamin Franklin, who flies kites when he's there according to Carpenter."

As soon as the wagon crossed Philadelphia's northern city limits and turned onto the Bristol Pike, they were confronted by a small British patrol.

"Halt", ordered the commander, who immediately dismounted and walked over to the wagon, sword in hand. In one fell swoop, he severed the main rope and pulled the tarp back. He moved a couple of seed bags and found a small keg covered in gunpowder dust. Again, with the sword, he popped open the lid, revealing the combustible contents.

The officer looked up at Pierre and Philip and announced, "We must confiscate this keg. You should be very thankful we don't arrest you and impound your wagon!"

"No, please wait sir. Our customer paid good money for that powder, and he needs it for hunting this winter," implored Pierre.

The officer pounded the lid back on and handed the keg to one of his men, who placed it in front of his saddle.

"As I said, you're both fortunate I'm letting you off so lightly. Now, be on your way before I have a change of heart!" He mounted his horse and galloped up the pike with his men following closely, disappearing behind a cloud of dust.

"That was close", said Philip as he jumped down from the wagon. "I'll re-secure the tarp."

They resumed their trip, hoping there would be no more interruptions or unintended consequences. Pierre asked Philip, "Do you know what that little keg was?"

"No, what?"

"That was our sacrificial lamb. They found what they were looking for, so the search was discontinued. Don't worry. We're not aiding and abetting the enemy because what appears to be gunpowder, is just coal powder mixed with flour. If our British friends try to use it, they won't even get a fizzle out of it, although they may be able to use the gunflour to bake a cake." Philip laughed bringing some relief to his ever-increasing tension and retorted, "Don't you mean gunflouder?"

Meanwhile, over in New Jersey, two men, Andrew Staleys and Thomas Ash, were leaving Batso Village iron works and furnace where iron was made from bog ore collected from of the shores of the nearby streams and rivers. They too manned a wagon with a false bottom hiding munitions and ammunition intended for the Continental Army congregating on the Pennsylvania side of the Delaware River. They were under strict orders to stay out of Titusville and camp close to the river all day on Christmas.

After their brush with the British patrol, Pierre and Philip made good time and arrived at Trevose, where Carpenter came out of Growden Mansion to greet them. A couple of his men unhitched the horses from the wagon and settled them into the barn. The weary travelers inspected the bunkhouse and rejoined Carpenter in the main house for a well-received meal and drinks. It was an enjoyable and relaxing evening, but they cut it short and sincerely thanked Carpenter for his hospitality. They retired early to be well-rested for Sunday's anticipated arrival at their destination.

By early afternoon, they pulled up to the Thompson-Neely house where they were immediately relieved of the wagon by a man who directed them into the Thompson side of the house and drove the rig into the barn. When the doors opened, Philip saw at least five horses still saddled milling about inside. Philip and Pierre had the home all to themselves and the stillness enabled them to hear the occasional agitated voices from the Neely side through the common wall. They remained together, but Pierre continually looked out the front window. Within the hour, he recognized a horseman quickly heading for the house. He stood up suddenly and hurriedly left the room, promising to return shortly. Pierre apologetically returned well over two hours later and explained that there had been complications that needed to be resolved. They were to remain indoors, and dinner would be brought to them, as well as breakfast the next morning. Philip got a distinct impression that he was the prisoner and Pierre was his guard. Pierre informed Philip that a horse would be tethered outside in the morning for his return to Philadelphia, and on his return to the city, he should leave the horse at the livery stable on Locust Street. The men retired early in the evening.

In the morning, they answered a persistent tapping on the door. A boy was not only delivering a big breakfast, but he also had a packed lunch for Philip too. The horse was already out front. They ate without much conversation as Philip was anxious to return home. He also knew that Pierre could not talk about the next phase of the plan, so he didn't persist.

"Pierre, I enjoyed being with you on this trip and I appreciate that you were forthcoming with me about the degree of risk. I'm relieved we've accomplished yet another successful expedition. I've never felt more alive than when I experienced the familiar fear I had while being confronted by those British soldiers and living through it. It brought back memories of our raid and confiscation of the Shawnee canoes. Thank you so much for asking me to join you and I wish you the best and much luck with what is next for you. I have just one question, my friend."

"What's that?", asked Pierre.

"For the last twenty hours or so, was I your prisoner?"

"But of course, I thought you'd never ask", answered Pierre. "Let's call it protective custody. In just a few days, the purpose of this adventure will become clear, and as promised at the outset, you will be enormously thrilled to have been strategically involved. Of that, I guarantee."

"Thank you. Until we meet again. Fare thee well."

"I'm looking forward to it already mon ami. One last thing, please don't ever forget me. I'll never forget you, Philippe."

"Same.", replied Philip.

They shook hands and Philip went outside. Now, a pure white stallion unlike any horse he had ever seen, was tied next to and towered over his horse. After admiring the beautiful animal, he got on his wagon horse and rode away in the direction of Philadelphia. He was on schedule to arrive later that day, in time for Christmas Eve to be with is darling Julia and Nathan too.

Christmas day, Wednesday, December 25, 1776, General George Washington left the Thompson-Neely house, later to be appropriately referred to as the

House of Decision. He mounted his favorite and most reliable steed and headed for the hidden camp. He assembled the officers and announced that this was the day they had been preparing for. They were to cross the Delaware River tonight, come ashore in Titusville, and head to British-occupied Trenton for a surprise attack. The targeted troops were German Hessian mercenary auxiliaries aiding the British under the command of Johann Rall.

The crossing was treacherous, with large chunks of ice flowing rapidly south in the strong current. The Continental Army, comprised of twenty-four hundred men, was accompanied by some enslaved people, including Prince Whipple, who was a soldier and bodyguard to General William Whipple, and Billy Lee, who was General Washington's personal assistant and valet. He was always by Washington's side during the battles. He would only leave to procure items much needed by the general, such as a stronger telescope. Billy Lee even successfully managed to obtain a replacement horse for Washington during the heat of one critical battle, which saved his life and allowed him to lead his troops to victory.

The Continental infantry and cavalry poled across the river in Durham boats, designed for heavy loads by the nearby Durham ironworks, along with a wide variety of watercraft that had been assembled just for this night. Ferry vessels were used for the large coaches, horses, and artillery. In addition to the initial crossing to surprise and rout the Hessians in the Battle of Trenton, there were two other crossings. One transported

British prisoners and military stores back to Pennsylvania. The other crossing returned to New Jersey to defeat the British reinforcements under Lord Cornwallis in the Second Battle of Trenton and to decimate his rear guard in the Battle of Princeton. These battles occurred during a period known as the Ten Crucial Days. The victories turned the tide of the war that would still rage on for another six-and-a-half years, officially ending on September 3rd, 1783. Ironically, the Peace Treaty of Paris 1763 ended the French Indian War, also known as the Seven Years War, and twenty years later, the Peace Treaty of Paris 1783 ended the war for American Independence.

I never imagined that my partnership with Alex would lead to such a wonderful friendship coupled with our remarkably lucrative partnership. I will never get over Pierre's surprise holiday visit and the resulting experience near the Delaware River. My life has been greatly enriched in many ways having known him. Will I ever see him again? I hope so, but I have a deep inclination that I will not.

October 1783

Chapter Eleven

Finally with the war over, Philip had closure on that unforgettable mission seven years before and he reflected upon it often. Pierre had been correct, in that Philip would experience enormous pride in his role. It had re-defined and emboldened him as an individual, profoundly enhancing his private and professional well-being. He never discussed his involvement with anyone except Julia, who always appreciated the fantastic story and the lasting effect it had on her husband. Philip could not resist writing about it extensively in his journal, which he held ever so private, even from Julia. She knew he made regular entries but she afforded it the same due respect for privacy that one gives to someone's personal diary.

The next decade passed by quickly and culminated in the Yellow Fever epidemic of 1793. Over those years, the business continued to flourish as did his relationship with Julia, whose parents were now deceased. Nathan, now in his early thirties, was out of the house. He was a sole practitioner because he could not possibly find a match with any of the firms in or around Philadelphia. He had purchased a townhouse in the two hundred block of Fifth Street and converted the first floor into his law office. Alex and Abbey also continued to enjoy the ongoing and growing contentment of a couple deeply in love. Their grown sons had joined the family business and were living nearby. Philip had always been grateful that Abbey found what she was looking for in his partner and best friend. Her father, who had become more and more curmudgeonly over time, was also long gone. Paul and Marion had taken over and were still operating the Man Full of Trouble Tavern, making a respectable living. Over the last seventeen years, Pierre had never contacted Philip and there had been no word from him by way of any other source. Philip understandably feared the worst, but he adamantly refused to give credence to these fears both mentally to himself and verbally to Julia. She too never brought up the subject in their many heart-to-heart conversations.

In the spring of 1793, oblivious to the more than fifty thousand people living in Philadelphia at the time, French colonial refugees arrived from Haiti on ships that also carried mosquitoes infected with the yellow fever virus. Five thousand Philadelphians would perish between August and November of that year, with twenty thousand fleeing the city in September.

Among those vacating the city was President Washington, who was renting a house at Sixth and Market Streets when Philadelphia was the temporary capital. He headed for his Mount Vernon estate, with his enslaved people Christopher Sheels, Oney Judge, Richmond, Giles, Austin, Paris, Hercules, Moll, and Joe. He would return to Philadelphia in November, and six years later, two years after his two-term presidency, Washington would die suddenly at age sixty-seven on December 14th, 1799. He specified in his will that his slaves were to be freed upon the death of his wife and he had established a fund to care for them.

In anticipation of celebrating their upcoming thirty-fifth wedding anniversary the next year, Philip had a special cabin constructed in his favorite ship TESORO for a surprise trip to Europe. He rejected the captain's offer to use his quarters in the stern of the ship so as not to undermine Captain William Palzell's authority. Philip also declined the services of his first mate Winston for that same reason. He and Julia would do just fine on their own. As it turned out, the new stateroom was completed early, so they were able to move the anniversary trip up, set sail for Europe in September, and escape the horrors of the epidemic. Alex and Philip had agreed earlier that Philip would use the trip to visit their business partners in the various ports-of-call. Alex would continue overseeing the Philadelphia operations remotely from the country estate he had inherited from his parents. Estranged son Nathan opted to remain in place and take his chances, which were excellent considering that he rarely came into direct contact with people, except for a few of his best clients.

The trip across the ocean was flawless much to the relief of Philip, whose past experiences left him skittish when he had to travel by ship, regardless of the distance or duration. Ships were now integral to his livelihood and sea travel was inevitable. Thank fortune for Alex, knowing of Philip's unseaworthy temperament, would often volunteer for the chore when the need presented itself. TESORO's cargo hold was empty allowing the hull to ride high in the water increasing the ship's speed considerably and rarely did she need to wait for strong winds.

Philip and Julia were thoroughly pleased with their accommodations. It was small, but comfortably furnished, including a real bed. Julia had instantly conformed to sea travel, and she was obviously enjoying the experience of life aboard ship. She was particularly amused when Captain Palzell would alter course, with the eager encouragement venting from Winston, to chase down a distant rainstorm. It would appear as a very dark, wide curtain extending from a gray cloud down to the horizon, in an otherwise azure, cloudless sky. The crew would dance shirtless while collecting the fresh water in barrels and any containers that could capture the precious universal solvent and lubricant of all bodily functions. Seeing Julia so happy took the edge off Philip's anxiety and made his seafaring days tolerable.

TESORO arrived at the first port, Lisbon, Portugal, in record time. As with all the ports, the host provided a carriage with a driver, a bedroom in his home, and delicious meals. The crew loaded the goods onto the ship, while the happy couple enjoyed a few days in and around the beautiful city of Lisbon. Philip expressed his elation at having both feet on solid ground, to which Julia joked that she would prefer to spend the nights back aboard the ship. After thoroughly exploring the city, they spent the following weeks in Malaga and La

Coruna, Spain, Le Havre and Paris, France, and Liverpool, England, before beginning the voyage home.

The return trip expectedly would take longer as TESORO was filled to capacity and the hull was submerged to its limit creating a drag that negatively impacted the ship's speed. Fortunately, the prevailing winds, ocean currents, and overall good weather conditions were favorable to their ever so slow progress westward. Much to the chagrin of Julia, detours to flirt with downpours were no longer on the itinerary. Philip and Julia enjoyed many new experiences and formed valued friendships, but they were thrilled to be returning home. Ships arriving from Philadelphia to Europe had carried the welcome news that the epidemic was subsiding. The mortality rate had peaked in October, and though not evident at the time, it was the frost that finally killed the infected mosquitoes in early November. The relieved, displaced residents began returning to their homes in droves.

Flushed with fond memories of their European tour, the Christmas season was exceptionally festive this year and filled with joyous times with friends and even family. Nathan displayed more personality than usual, and he even aspired to initiate conversations with his parents. He was still alone, with no apparent prospects on the horizon. Philip didn't share his growing consternation with anyone, but he had a persistent feeling that times seemed too good. The favorable present seemed to be setting the stage for entry into an ominous future. It was hard for him to fathom that seventeen years had now gone by since he parted ways with Pierre. He was haunted by their last verbal exchange promising not to forget each other. Philip now knew that the parting had been a genuine exitrant. He was thankful for being spared the raw, painful emotions he would have experienced if he had known, at that time, it was a final separation. Over the next several years, recurrences of yellow fever surfaced in Baltimore in 1794, and in New York in 1795, followed by outbreaks in Wilmington, and Boston. A new variant of the virus unexpectedly surfaced in Philadelphia in 1798. It chose victims indiscriminately and attacked mercilessly.

I never thought that I would grow old. It sneaks up on you. I notice that time passes exponentially faster every year as one ages, in direct correlation to the fewer new experiences encountered, and earmark memories registered by those of us who are older.

January 1798

Chapter Twelve

Julia contracted the fever and was dead in three days. Philip was devastated beyond words and he simply could not write of her passing in his journal or express the agonizing pain of the sadness he felt during the few days leading up to her death. That painful sadness exploded into unimaginable grief when she died in his arms and his mourning for her would be endless.

The day after the service and funeral at Pine Street Church was unlike any he had ever experienced. On awakening, he totally forgot that Julia had died and then reality crashed back into his mind, overwhelming him with nausea. Although he had nowhere to go, he had to leave the lonely house. He forced himself to get up and put one foot in front of the other. He had slept in his clothes, so he slowly walked directly to the front door and went out into the bleak day. He had no destination but ended up where he and Julia used to picnic when they were young and so in love. On that site now stood the new courthouse that was connected by a covered breezeway to the west side of Independence Hall. He sat down on a granite slab at the backdoor used by the barristers. There was already a pronounced indentation in the slab where they would step when entering and leaving the courthouse. He looked south down Sixth Street and recalled the hours they had spent watching those enjoying the pond that was now gone. Men were beginning construction on a brick wall that would surround the former Potter's Field, now named Southeast Square. Thoughts of Julia gave way to other memories.

The human psyche never ages and it makes one feel ageless and forever young until it eventually leads to the inevitable rude awakening of being old. The saving grace is that all living creatures have the commonality of aging and dying. Misery loves company. The psyche is also extremely complex, resilient, and mind controlling. Sitting there alone, his thoughts began a downward spiral to the past and suddenly emblazoned in his mind were the images of his dead parents and sister. For many years, he could not assemble clear details of their faces. He now saw their faces exactly how they looked before being murdered. The memory of their violent deaths didn't trigger any emotions in him at all. Time heals.

Pierre was the next uninvited guest to the mental review. Philip pictured Claude negotiating with Bear in a very agitated fashion but ending on a good note. Slowly Pierre's face disappeared and the faces of Mr. and Mrs. Hopkins were presented to him by his brain. He knew they were gone, but their presence was always with him. Their introduction into his young and desperate life could not have come at a better time.

Old man McCorkle invaded his stream of semi-consciousness and thankfully he was quickly displaced by Abbey and Paul. He had lost touch with Paul, but he had seen Abbey regularly with Alex. Their personal secret regarding that night had remained just that—secret. When Alex and his father flashed through his head, he just smiled.

His imagination then placed him aboard a rapidly sinking ship with four captains on the bridge—Gramond, Tarrant, Palzell, and of course, Brackett, whose face was rotted by saltwater. That scene was replaced by a gathering of his European friends, and again, he smiled with delight. That delight was rudely shattered by the intrusion of the recollection of Nathan's unemotional demeanor at his mother's memorial service and funeral. That thought snapped him out of his mental state and freed his mind from his overactive psyche. Physically and mentally exhausted from the past week, he stood up to leave. Not knowing, or caring, that he would be dead in less than a year, he walked back to a home that now appeared to him totally differently. With no interest in food, he headed for his bed for the welcome escape of sleep, but first, he wrote what would be his next to last entry in his journal.

My grief of losing you is a horrible reminiscence of the days I lost my family. I miss you so much. Nothing could ever replace you. I will always love you more my dear Julia. Your life is spent, as is mine until I hold you again when I go home.

June 1798

Chapter Thirteen

A life of too much rich food and fine wine led to advanced coronary artery disease and occasional flare-ups of gout. Philip's faltering mind produced thoughts that became increasingly morbid. He lay in bed and mused that the only thing one does completely alone is die. Even when you're born, your mother is present. He murmured aloud to himself, "When you're dead, do you know if you have ever lived?"

In reply to visitor inquires as to his health, he would gloss over his obvious deteriorating condition, with a standard reply, "Most everything that ills me is age-related. Stenosis in my neck, accompanied by four herniated disks, high-pitched hearing loss, floaters, cataracts, macular degeneration, assorted bruises, and a diminished, but frequent, urine stream. I consider myself fortunate to have lived long enough to enable the development of these timely, but most unwelcome ailments, for which my body lives to be their host. They have left their mark on my soul like the concentric age-rings within the trunk of an old tree. Surely there are now a few dormant, undiagnosed surprises awaiting the opportunity to manifest themselves in my aged bark." He would typically conclude his comments by reciting the Shakespearian quote: "With the mirth and laughter of youth, let old wrinkles come."

Philip also endured an arthritic right knee, bursitis in his right hip, a torn bicep tendon in his right inner elbow, a double-jointed right shoulder, ringing in his right ear, and a right bundle branch block in his heart. All his maladies were on the right side. When friends asked, "How do you feel?", he would reply, "All right, but my old, used-up body will soon be all that's left." He was internally pleased with himself when he punned the words all right to be homonymous with the word alright. Oh, the little pleasures in life.

After his best friend Alex had tearfully left the bedside, the next and final visitor was a dry-eyed Nathan, to whom Philip gave his journal with the lone request that he read it cover to cover and try to get something out of it. Later that day in his law office, Nathan read a handful of entries, lost interest, and inattentively shelved the journal in his library, ignoring his father's dying request. It blended in with a menagerie of legal tomes and would remain unnoticed for many years. After a thirty-two-year career, he sold his library to James Scarlett, Esq., who subsequently sold the books to a traveling used law book salesman, who canvased Pennsylvania, in his wagon. Thus, began the transport of a concealed journal into the future where it would not be discovered for another one hundred and seventy years.

On June 13, 1799, at age sixty-one, Philip Winemore Ambruster died alone, sitting up in bed with his journal on his lap, quill in his hand, smile on his face, and Julia on his mind. The day had entered the second, and final two golden hours and the sunset was beginning to yield to the civil, nautical, and astronomical twilights to be followed by nighttime. A cardinal that had lingered outside his window on a branch all day long suddenly flew away. Shortly before he drew his last breath, rapid eye movement began behind his eyelids releasing a single tear that slowly rolled down his cheek. He smiled slightly and whispered, "I love *you* more." At the exact moment of his death, the sun slid below the horizon producing a bright green flash. This natural phenomenon was caused by the combination of a mirage and the dispersion of sunlight. Some would contend that the brilliant instantaneous display was also a supernatural recognition and celebration of a life well lived.

It would be determined later that a blockage had exacerbated his congestive heart failure. In reality, Philip's heart had been broken since Julia had died the year before, causing him terminal sadness with relief only when Julia would periodically visit him in his dreams. Philip was laid to rest next to his beloved Julia as the sun was burning through the morning mist in the burial ground of Pine Street Church near Fourth Street. They were together again just inside the front east gate, to the left of the cemetery sidewalk, on the right side of the first sycamore tree. As per his request, the service was brief but entertaining because those in attendance were thoroughly amused by his self-composed epitaph engraved on the tomb slab that was carefully placed on top of the red-brick grave box:

> My life is spent, its path is run
> My soul in a new state is God's
> I once stood where now you be
> So prepare with speed to follow me

As the mourners dispersed, a lone figure remained at the gravesite, immobilized by her innermost thoughts, memories, and deep emotions. She was obviously well-to-do, as evidenced by her stylish clothing. An eagle-feathered hairpiece was pinned to her long, braided hair. Her stance suggested an eloquent and self-assured demeanor. The finest of carriages awaited her, with a set of powerful stallions still breathing hard and sweating excessively from the long, fast trip they had just completed. Sarah Remington, a widow of some years, had just heard of the existence of her brother and his terminal condition, and she rushed to Philadelphia overnight.

She was at a luncheon in New York City, including some attendees from Philadelphia, when she overheard them discussing that one of their friends, who is a well-known businessman, was sadly on his deathbed. She distinctly heard the name Ambruster, and on further inquiry, she learned his name was Philip. On gathering more information from the Philadelphians, Sarah ascertained that the dying man was her brother. She immediately exited the hotel, entered her carriage, and began the trip to Philadelphia. Sarah arrived at his home early the next morning and was directed to the church. It was now impossible for her to reconcile with her brother, who she assumed had perished along

I ONCE STOOD

with her parents on that terrible night so many years ago. The details of her life, from that fateful night to the present, which she had intended to share with Philip, would have to remain solely Sarah's story—for now. But then again, unlike her brother, Sarah had not maintained a personal journal. Or did she?

All things considered, I've had a good life and I'm having a decent death. I was blessed to have grown old with the woman I truly love. The question is—will I awake at first light or draw my last breath? Another question—will Nathan mourn for me?

As I contemplate my imminent demise, I trust I've earned a panel in the quilt of former lives that will warm, comfort, and perhaps amuse those who remember me within that patchwork of random souls blanketing out for all of eternity. I'm tired. It's time to close my book.

June 12, 1799

Epilogue

George T. Bisel Company, Inc., a Pennsylvania law book publishing house located in the southwest corner of Washington Square, Philadelphia, was founded by its namesake, in 1876. Mr. Bisel initially traveled throughout Pennsylvania selling law blanks, stationery, and used law books to the profession. Today, the company, managed by the sixth generation of Bisel family members, publishes its own line of Pennsylvania-specific titles for distribution to law libraries across the country in addition to e-books, downloads, and live online accessibility to cases. Over the years, Mr. Bisel bought out all seven of his competitors, including their extensive inventories, which included books printed by Benjamin Franklin. In a published nineteenth-century photograph, one of these rival companies T. & J.W. Johnson's building, with a sign advertising "LAW BOOKS", can clearly be seen directly across the street from Independence Hall.

Upon his arrival in Philadelphia, Mr. Bisel rented space on Lawyers' Row, comprised of former residential eighteenth-century townhouses, at Sixth and Walnut Streets. Subsequently, he leased space in five locations in the seven hundred block of Sansom Street, referred to as Jewelers' Row. In 1948, the company leased and eventually bought the building on Washington Square, also known as Publishers' Row. Today, the company is the only surviving publisher on the square. The Bisel family attributes the company's success and longevity to a clause in George T. Bisel's will stipulating that ten percent of all profits be distributed to a Christian ministry.

The six-story brick building at 710 South Washington Square originally served as a warehouse for the Henry Dreer Seed Company, Schuylkill Paper Company, and later for the Farm Journal Publishing Company. Except for the two basements and the top three floors, the building was renovated inside and out. White marble steps lead up to an ornate doorframe, with the company name engraved above the door in ten-carat gold leaf. The interior features a leaded glass vestibule and the public floors are replete with oriental rugs, elaborate wainscoting, genuine wood paneling, ornate crown molding, and brass chandeliers. A tenfoot solid oak conference table graces the boardroom. The walls have large watercolor paintings of buildings in Washington D.C., engravings of historical sites in Philadelphia, and of course, a row of presidential portraits starting with George T. Bisel. The most compelling space in the building is the top, sixth floor. It is similar to floors four and five with no heat or air conditioning and lighting provided by bare, incandescent lightbulbs tangling at the end of original electric wires.

Only the sixth floor is home to thousands of books from the bare wooden floor to the ceiling, with exposed structural beams. The front and back walls have four windows overlooking the square in the front and the alley in the rear. The brick side walls support wide shelves and a long five-foot wide wooden platform takes up the center of the floor, from front to back. The front quarter of the floor serves as the Bisel archives containing two copies of every book ever published by the company. The rest of the center platform is home to stack after stack of the books obtained early on when Mr. Bisel traveled Pennsylvania in his wagon buying and selling law libraries. The books acquired from his competitors, including the large Benjamin Franklin volumes are covered by an old, dirty plastic sheet. The side wall shelves are packed with sidebar reports, Fiduciary Reporter volumes, and miscellaneous bound law books, with the traditional red and black bands, on the spines.

* * *

Upon graduation from college, the young man started with Bisel Company in 1974 and he was assigned to the shipping department because it was the busy season. He eventually discovered the treasures of the sixth floor. He spent many lunchtime breaks perusing the old volumes, especially the Benjamin Franklin books, with non-yellowed acid free paper. The title page of one particular volume reads: "*Votes and Proceedings of the House of Representatives of the Province of Pennsylvania beginning the fourteenth day of October 1726. Printed and Sold by B. Franklin and D. Hall, at the New Printing Office, near the Market.*" The referenced House of Representatives met in the State

House, which would later be known as Independence Hall. One day, he removed that book from the stack and opened it. He was perplexed to find leaves and ferns inside the book being pressed between some of the pages. As his career advanced, he spent less time in the stacks until a day in 1982 when he read an article about Benjamin Franklin in National Geographic. The piece included information that caught his attention and made him catch his breath. It read, "When Benjamin Franklin had the contract to print the minutes of the State House proceedings, he also had the contract to print the colonial money. To thwart counterfeiting, Franklin would imprint the image of leaves and ferns on the paper money."

He immediately bolted to the freight elevator, the oldest in Philadelphia, and rose to the sixth floor, opened the Franklin book, inspected the ferns to discover they were identical to the ferns imprinted on the currency featured in the magazine. After getting permission, he relocated the Franklin volumes to a large closest on the heated and air conditioned second floor, with special attention paid to the fern book. He returned upstairs to clean up the wooden platform where the books had been and to ditch the old plastic sheet. He noticed a large, brown book that had not been visible before. It was wedged between two stacks of normal-sized law books, but he was able to retrieve it without damaging the old book. He opened the front cover and saw that the first page contained an elaborate personalized inscription written in a dramatic, sweeping script. He turned to the next page featuring well-spaced sentences in meticulous penmanship, making the entries effortless to read. He read aloud—*I was born in 1738 in a cabin deep in the western Virginia wilderness.* After reading dozens of pages of personal handwritten entries in the book, he had an idea. He would blend the journal entries into a storyline and expand the journal's contents into a novel based on fact. As spare time allowed, he spent the balance of 1982 working on the manuscript by pounding out the journal's contents, along with embellishments, page by page, on his IBM Selectic typewriter. With mounting responsibilities, there was less time to spend on the project and it was "temporarily" set aside for the next ten years. He inserted the manuscript and some loose pages into a black three-ring binder, and carefully wrapped the journal in brown paper. They were both placed in the deep bottom drawer of his gray metal desk. The next time he would have any contact with his manuscript and the journal was a decade later in 1992 when he became CEO and moved into the executive office. He transferred the binder and journal into a cabinet in his new office, where they would remain untouched for another twenty-eight years.

During the winter of 2020, he began to clean out and organize his office in anticipation of perhaps considering the ever-so-popular COVID-19 pandemic-inspired retirement—a self-imposed syndrome to which he ultimately would not succumb. In one of the built-in cabinets under shelves of law books covering an entire wall, he re-discovered his black three-ring binder. It was under a pile of aging, dusty documents next to a large rectangular brown package. He sat on the oriental rug in front of the wall of law books, surrounded by antique furniture, clocks, and lamps. The other three walls held portraits and old photographs of the Bisel family, who silently bore witness to him opening the binder. It contained the first draft of the 1982 manuscript he put away in 1992, twenty-eight years prior. The first half of the manuscript consisted of several chapters complete with a storyline and sketchy dialog. The second half held single sheets for each chapter, with chapter headings and summaries, as if copied from a diary, waiting to be expanded. The binder also contained hand-written notes, brochures of historic Philadelphia sites, and a general timeline. A list of supporting character names to be added to the actual names in the journal had been copied from tombstones in local Philadelphia church graveyards.

As he read the thirty-eight-year-old typed pages, he felt as if he was reading someone else's work. He didn't recall any of the story on the old typewritten pages, although he knew he had done the typing. At close to age sixty-eight, he decided to rekindle the effort that he had begun at age thirty by re-typing the IBM Selectric typewriter's manuscript, word for word, plus enhancements, into a modern DELL laptop computer. That weekend, he resumed a project that would take him until May 2024 to complete, a span of forty-two years, by keying in the words from the original 1982 manuscript's Title Page—**"I Once Stood."**

About the Author

Franklin Jon Zuch was born and raised in Pennsylvania. Born on May 3rd, 1952, he toddled in a small Cape Cod-style home in Morton and was raised in Delaware County, with an older brother and three younger sisters. His father was Herman Franklin Zuch, Jr. from York, and his mother was Erma Jane Snavely from Lancaster. Herman and Erma chose to go by Frank and Jane, but they knew they were meant for each other because Erma is in the name Herman. Through his mother's lineage, Mr. Zuch is related to milk chocolate candy mogul, Milton Snavely Hershey. He started his candy business with Aunt Mattie at Tenth and Spring Garden Streets in Philadelphia, specializing in caramel. Milton Hershey, who lost interest and money in the caramel venture, re-directed his efforts toward milk chocolate. He moved the business to Lancaster County because, as he would say, "That's where the cows are."

Mr. Zuch received a Bachelor of Arts degree in Political Science from Villanova University, married George T. Bisel's great, great, granddaughter Judy in 1973, and in 1974, he accepted a job in the shipping department of the George T. Bisel Company, law publishers, on Washington Square, Philadelphia. His career would span half a century, with thirty-two years as CEO. Judy and Frank lived in an apartment in Chestnut Hill until the birth of the first of their two daughters compelled them to buy a Neshaminy Valley townhouse in Bensalem. In 2001, they bought their dream summer home in Ocean City, New Jersey, and in 2012 moved Down the Shore full time.

Mr. Zuch's past and present affiliations include Friends of Growden Mansion, where Benjamin Franklin flew his famous kite, the Pennsylvania Historical Society, Philadelphia Book Clinic, The Pennsylvania Society, Langhorne Presbyterian Church, Ocean City Tabernacle, and the Union League of Philadelphia.

In retirement, the Zuchs spend the winter in their Bradenton, Florida villa on a private road surrounded by IMG Academy's golf course. They continue to spend summers at their home in Ocean City. Over the years, they were blessed with four grandchildren—three extraordinary young men and a young lady, who has a penchant for pageants and she has the rhinestone-studded crowns to prove it.